The insistent bleat of  **ness of Taylor's cabin.**

She bolted upright in bed, her feet dropping to the cool floor. She stared at the green LED digits on her clock radio—the lights glowered rudely at her: 4:22 a.m. Why was she getting a call for a medevac at that hour? She wasn't on nighttime call that week. Taylor fell back on her pillow and fumbled for the receiver. "Yes?" she croaked.

"Taylor, wake up. It's me." When she recognized the voice of Nate Mueller, she sat up again in surprise. "We got trouble. I just got a call from the troopers. Center reported losing a King Air. It was two-three-two. It dropped off . . .

A knot formed in her gut. Taylor mentally ran down the list of pilots on standby that night, and realized Erica was one of them. She had given Erica a brief pep talk not nine hours earlier when a medevac had been dispatched, and the younger woman was slated to be on the crew that took that flight. She had been excited—her first duty call.

MORE MYSTERIES FROM THE
BERKLEY PUBLISHING GROUP...

CHINA BAYLES MYSTERIES: She left the big city to run an herb shop in Pecan Springs, Texas. But murder can happen anywhere... "A wonderful character!"   —*Mostly Murder*

by Susan Wittig Albert

THYME OF DEATH   WITCHES' BANE
HANGMAN'S ROOT   ROSEMARY REMEMBERED
RUEFUL DEATH   LOVE LIES BLEEDING

KATE JASPER MYSTERIES: Even in sunny California, there are cold-blooded killers... "This series is a treasure!"   —Carolyn G. Hart

by Jacqueline Girdner

ADJUSTED TO DEATH   MURDER MOST MELLOW
THE LAST RESORT   FAT-FREE AND FATAL
TEA-TOTALLY DEAD   A STIFF CRITIQUE
MOST LIKELY TO DIE   A CRY FOR SELF-HELP
DEATH HITS THE FAN
(available in hardcover from Berkley Prime Crime)

BONNIE INDERMILL MYSTERIES: Temp work can be murder, but solving crime is a full-time job... "One of detective fiction's most appealing protagonists!"   —*Publishers Weekly*

by Carole Berry

THE DEATH OF A DIFFICULT WOMAN   GOOD NIGHT, SWEET PRINCE
THE LETTER OF THE LAW   THE DEATH OF A DANCING FOOL
THE YEAR OF THE MONKEY   DEATH OF A DIMPLED DARLING

MARGO SIMON MYSTERIES: She's a reporter for San Diego's public radio station. But her penchant for crime solving means she has to dig up the most private of secrets...

by Janice Steinberg

DEATH OF A POSTMODERNIST   DEATH CROSSES THE BORDER
DEATH-FIRES DANCE   THE DEAD MAN AND THE SEA

EMMA RHODES MYSTERIES: She's a "Private Resolver," a person the rich and famous can turn to when a problem needs to be resolved quickly and quietly. All it takes is $20,000 and two weeks for Emma to prove her worth... "Fast...clever...charming." —*Publishers Weekly*

by Cynthia Smith

NOBLESSE OBLIGE   IMPOLITE SOCIETY
MISLEADING LADIES

DEAD STICK

Megan Mallory Rust

BERKLEY PRIME CRIME, NEW YORK

To William,
whose great suggestions launched a successful endeavor.

DEAD STICK

A Berkley Prime Crime Book / published by arrangement with
the author

PRINTING HISTORY
Berkley Prime Crime edition / May 1998

The Penguin Putnam Inc. World Wide Web site address is
http://www.penguinputnam.com

ISBN: 0-425-16296-6

Berkley Prime Crime Books are published by
The Berkley Publishing Group,
a member of Penguin Putnam Inc.,
200 Madison Avenue, New York, NY 10016.
The name BERKLEY PRIME CRIME and the
BERKLEY PRIME CRIMEdesign are trademarks
belonging to Berkley Publishing Corporation.

PRINTED IN THE UNITED STATES OF AMERICA

10 9 8 7 6 5 4 3 2 1

ACKNOWLEDGMENTS

M any of my friends in the Alaskan aviation and medical communities were kind enough to assist me on the technical details of *Dead Stick,* and deserve a round of applause.

Margaret Auble, RN, director of Lifeguard Alaska, was generous with her time and knowledge of medical evacuations; Bill Berson, A&P, IA, my favorite aircraft mechanic, always had a reply when I asked, "What if ... ," and came up with some great ideas; Jim LaBelle, chief of the Alaskan division of the National Transportation Safety Board (NTSB), and George Kobelnyk, NTSB air safety investigator, answered my questions like the pros they are; Don Rogers, MD, State of Alaska Medical Examiner (he of the gory photos), patiently addressed medical topics so that a layperson like myself could follow; Jon Sutherlin, King Air B200 captain for Lifeguard Alaska, refreshed my memory on some aeronautical details, and threw in some arcane minutiae of his own; Clint Swanson, director of maintenance for Rust's Flying Service, used his devious mind to invent ways to destroy King Airs, and told me about them; Hank Rust, my dad, was an always-present encyclopedia of aviation facts, and if the questions weren't too stupid (and sometimes when they were), he'd offer the answers to them.

For those I forgot to mention—and you know who you are—my heartfelt thanks. Without the help of my friends, I couldn't have created believable characters and situations, and I'm deeply indebted to you.

ONE

Ten fifty-nine p.m.

Taylor Morgan squinted at her wristwatch, shrugged, and rolled her jacket cuff back down. Her gaze returned forward to the Plexiglas windshield of the Beechcraft King Air B200. Even with midnight only an hour away, the image filling the twin-engine turboprop's windshield showed clouds still tinged pink by a sun barely hidden by the horizon.

Another August evening in Alaska was ending.

Taylor turned to stare out the aircraft's side window. To her left rose the urban skyline of downtown Anchorage, the golden birch thickets beyond the city's outskirts losing their color in the fading daylight. To the east, the rugged 6,500-foot peaks of the Chugach Mountains stood silhouetted against indigo skies. To the north and west, the waters of Cook Inlet and Knik Arm dulled to a monochromatic dark gray.

Taylor looked away from the window and turned toward the woman seated to her right: Erica Wolverton, her copilot. She saw a pair of cornflower-blue eyes locked in intense concentration below a cluster of strawberry-blond curls reminiscent of Lil' Orphan Annie. The lights on the instrument panel reflected from the lenses of her aviator-style glasses. The woman's tall, gangly body was nearly motionless, with only her long, slender fingers showing activity as they flexed and relaxed, over and over, against the aircraft's control yoke.

That picture made Taylor smile. In the past, she had been similarly tense when *she* was a new copilot learning the routine for medical evacuation flights in the King Air. As a complete neophyte, she had a lot to learn. In addition, as a woman working at a job traditionally held by a man, she felt pressure to prove her competency. *Especially* to the check pilot, invariably male, who evaluated her.

She hoped the younger woman found it easier to perform well in front of a female check pilot. Perhaps Erica Wolverton was actually enjoying the check ride. She hoped so—she'd never flown with another woman as part of a flight crew, and she certainly liked the change.

After another moment of rumination, she shook her head and got back to business. "It's getting kinda late. I guess I'll take that hood off you. We've done enough for tonight." She reached out to grab the plastic visor wrapped around her copilot's forehead.

Erica sighed as her curls slipped out from underneath the hood's headband. "That thing left welts on me," she grumbled, then chuckled in a contralto timbre. "Maybe we could try a pair of really dark wraparound sunglasses next time."

The arch of Taylor's eyebrows signaled her appreciation of her companion's jest. "I'm sure they make a hood that doesn't stripe your face, Erica, but I guess the company didn't want to put a lot of money into something they wouldn't use much. There's plenty of days when we can't even see the ground from two hundred feet, so why fake it with a hood?" She juggled the almond-colored plastic shield in her hands and glanced down at the instrument panel. "Anyway, make this a full stop."

The other pilot nodded and pressed the push-to-talk button on her control yoke to activate her boom mike. "Anchorage tower, two-three-two-lima-lima is turning final for six-right, full stop this time."

"Two-three-two-lima-lima, Anchorage, cleared to land on six-right, traffic is a JAL 747 crossing six-left at kilo, contact ground on point nine upon exiting the runway."

"Two-lima-lima copies, cleared to land, six-right." Erica released the button and aimed her next words at her captain. "Still my ship?" she asked.

"Yup, still yours, show me a real greaser this time. Imagine you've got a critical case behind you that's not going to appreciate a bouncy landing." She cinched down her seat belt and grinned, lacing her fingers behind her head.

Smiling in turn, Erica prepared the aircraft for its imminent touchdown.

Out of the corner of her eye Taylor saw her depress the wheel-shaped lever that lowered the landing gear. When Erica fumbled with the lever, raising and lowering it several more times, she swung around to focus on her copilot's activity. "We got a problem?" she said, frowning.

"Yeah"—Erica poked at a trio of green lights marked DOWN AND LOCKED—"we've definitely got a problem. The gear's not coming down. The lights aren't burned out, but I still don't have three green showing."

"Oh, damn," Taylor groaned. "It's probably just an intermittent twitch in the electrical system. Let's slow down, see if we get a horn."

When the other woman slid the power levers back, an answering shriek confirmed the problem. Any time the engine power was decreased below a certain level, without the landing gear extended, a shrill alarm sounded.

A lump shot up Taylor's throat when she heard the wail of the warning horn. Their landing gear really hadn't come down. She'd never had an actual emergency in any of the planes she flew, and certainly not during a copilot checkout flight. The emergencies she'd seen were only simulations, created to test a pilot's ability to handle one.

But she hadn't planned this one.

"Okay, start the emergency checklist; I'll notify tower we're going around. I've got it." With adrenaline coursing through her veins, Taylor grabbed the controls, pushed the power levers forward again, and spoke into her mike. "Anchorage tower, two-lima-lima has a gear problem; we're going around until we get it fixed."

A few seconds passed without an answer from the tower, and she knew the controller was looking at her airplane through his binoculars, assessing the situation.

"Yeah, I've got you in sight," replied the controller. "Your gear doors are open, but nothing's down. Stay up at pattern altitude until you've got 'em down and locked."

"Two-lima-lima copies." Taylor deactivated her boom mike and squinted out her side window. This problem could be trouble—if they couldn't get the gear down, the consequences could be devastating. The King Air could pancake onto the runway and skid down the asphalt on its unprotected belly. Extensive damage to the aircraft body and engines could result. She shuddered.

Then she shook herself away from those ideas. Nothing would happen; she was trained to handle emergencies like that. She should just make the best of the situation.

Turning back toward Erica, she pointed at the gear handle. Matter-of-factly she said, "Okay, let's get this cleaned up. What does the emergency checklist say?" Butterflies still fluttered in her stomach, but she decided to ignore them. She'd be cool, act like this was no big deal. Evaluate her *copilot's* response to the situation, not her own.

The drawn features on Erica's face told her that the other woman was feeling some anxiety, too. Quite likely, this was her first taste of an unplanned emergency in a complex aircraft. In addition, she didn't have Taylor's experience in the plane, couldn't gauge the severity of the situation.

How would Erica conduct herself? That would serve to be her first test as a new flight crew member.

Flipping to the proper section of the checklist, Erica glanced at it perfunctorily and began reading. "First, confirm the problem and reduce speed. Then, disable the landing gear relay by pulling its circuit breaker." She glanced over at her captain. "Go ahead and do that, I'll lower the gear handle again. Next step is cranking the gear down by hand." She bent over toward the floor of the cockpit and began pumping a lever. She'd obviously taken a hold of herself and the situation. Her words were unwavering and precise, and it appeared she knew the emergency sequences by heart.

Along with muffled grunts from her partner, a subtle grinding noise filled the cockpit and Taylor could feel the King Air's reaction to the landing gear extension. The gear was coming down.

She drew a deep breath, unaware that she had been holding it.

A short time later Erica poked her head up and declared the job done. "I got three green now, all we gotta do is confirm it with the tower in a fly-by." She reached to key her mike, then hesitated. "You want me to do that, or did you want to?"

"No, go ahead. Looks like you've got everything under control." Taylor smiled. She'd underestimated the slender woman next to her—if Erica had been nervous about her first emergency, her voice and actions hadn't shown it.

Sitting back in her seat, she watched her copilot complete the flight.

The silver-and-burgundy King Air crunched over a scattering of gravel as Erica guided it onto an asphalt parking area. The vertical tail of the aircraft displayed the logo of LifeLine Air Ambulance, the medical evacuation company that employed both pilots. The rotating beacon on the top of the tail intermittently stained the decal below crimson.

Most of the day's activities on the parking ramp had

ended by that time, though a small blue-and-white aircraft tug still maneuvered about the area, headed for the King Air's intended destination.

By the time Taylor had the aircraft's engines spooling down, the tug's driver had connected a towing harness to its nose wheel. When he stepped back and gave a thumbs-up sign, the two women slipped out of their cockpit seats and walked back to the rear cabin door.

"Well, I'm beat," Taylor cracked. "I don't know who worked harder tonight, you or me. Copilot checks are tough, even for the captain. Especially with emergencies thrown in." She rolled her eyes in mock exasperation and reached for the latch on the rear cabin door. Even though she tried to look nonchalant, she knew her smile told her companion she had been pleased with the outcome of the flight.

With a jerk on the latch and a shove the airstair opened. A hydraulic *swoosh!* stirred the air as the heavy stairs slowly swung out and down from the cabin like the emergence of a robot's arm.

A cool summer evening breeze wafted into the stuffy cabin, cleaning the stale air and prompting Erica to breathe in deeply. "Nice night, huh? I can enjoy it now."

"Was the check ride that bad? I thought it would be easier riding with me than a man."

Then she realized what Erica had been stressed *by,* and rested her hand on the woman's shoulder. "Hey, you did real good with that gear problem; you've been studying your emergency procedures." She dropped her hand and gestured for the other woman to follow her down the airstairs. "I gotta go into the office, call the mechanic. He's gotta come in tonight and check the gear on two-three-two. That ship has to be ready if a medevac call comes in."

As they trotted down the airstair, she decided to voice what she had been thinking most of the night. "You know, Erica, it's kinda fun flying with you. I've never flown with another female pilot before, but I really like it. You've got a good soft touch with the airplane. Some guys are so rough with it.''

Upon reaching the asphalt she halted and turned toward the waiting tug. ''Hey, Doug,'' she yelled at the teenage tug driver, ''I'll open the hangar doors when we get inside, go ahead and roll two-three-two into its spot, okay?''

The boy unconsciously pushed a hank of his longish, shaggy hair out of his eyes and waved to confirm her comment. ''Right, Taylor,'' he yelled back in a hesitant baritone voice. ''I'll take care of it, you can split after the doors are open. See you later!''

Shaking her head, she beckoned to the other woman. ''I swear,'' she whispered, ''every time I hear that kid his voice is different. Earlier today, he sounded like Tiny Tim singing 'Tiptoe Through the Tulips' and then tonight he sounds like Pavarotti. Aren't you glad our voices didn't change like that when we were teenagers? The boys must feel like real dips, squeaking one hour and croaking the next.''

''Yeah, right. Like we didn't have trouble when *we* were growing up? I can still remember crying over not having a bra, like I was the only one without any tits.''

''Yeah, I did the same thing.'' Taylor glanced down at her chest as though she was back in junior high.

Satisfied that she still filled out her shirt adequately, she unlocked the hangar door and flicked on the lights. Her sneakered feet created little sound as she crossed the hangar, but Erica's hiking boots produced heavy clonking footsteps.

''So, what do you think about these?'' Taylor asked, swinging her arm from one side of the building to the other. Her gesture encompassed the rest of the LifeLine's fleet— the twin of the King Air they had just flown and a single Learjet. ''I bet that Lear's why you applied for a job here, huh?''

Before the younger woman had a chance to answer, Taylor triggered the button that activated the opening of the hangar doors. The heavy, wide slabs began to slide apart, groaning like the keyboards of a mammoth accordion. A Boeing 727 growled in accompaniment during its liftoff from nearby Runway Six-Left. Fading light filtered through the spreading doors.

The *put-put-put* of the tug pulling their King Air into the hangar joined in with the other noises, and Erica raised her voice to compete. "No, it wasn't the chance of flying the Lear that attracted me. My other job was driving me nuts, and I needed some excitement in my life."

"Well, we sure get excitement here from time to time." Taylor watched the tug driver maneuver their aircraft into its assigned hangar parking slot and then flipped the door operation toggle again. The harsh incandescent beams from spotlights in the ceiling replaced the soft natural light, and she continued her hike across the hangar toward the LifeLine office. "You know, I read your résumé. You said you worked for Central Alaska Express. Copilot, on a Beech 1900. That's a pretty cool airplane. How'd you get bored?" Without a doubt, she would have loved flying a ship like that when *she* had started out.

"Oh, it wasn't the 1900 that bored me, it was where I flew it. I had the same schedule every day: Anchorage to Kenai, Kenai to Homer, Homer to Anchorage, Anchorage to Kenai . . . blah, blah, blah. Basically, that's a bus driver's schedule. I wanted something more interesting, like a job as a medevac pilot." She nodded emphatically.

When the two women reached the far side of the hangar they stepped into a small room. Taylor flipped on lights that revealed a row of gray lockers and a wooden bench. Wide bands of adhesive tape mounted on the lockers held names—Price, Derossett, Sosnowski, McNiven, Morgan. She opened her locker and dropped a notebook next to the black leather flight bag at the bottom. On the top shelf a pair of mirrored sunglasses glinted in the light; a small clear plastic container holding foam earplugs dangled from a neighboring hook.

"Has Nate found you a Nomex flight suit yet?" Taylor asked.

When Erica shook her head, Taylor pointed at the light-weight navy blue coveralls hanging inside her locker. "Nate had to make a special order for these; everything they had lying around the office was too long for me." She eyed the other woman's lanky, slender form. "That won't be a problem for you, though. If anything, it'll be long enough, but way too big across."

Turning to her right, toward another door, she flipped the locker room lights off as she entered LifeLine's front office. The plate glass windows on one wall allowed entrance to what remained of the dusky evening. She stepped up to a phone nested in a pile of papers. "Nate's not too neat, huh?" she complained as she straightened some of the papers and set them aside.

As Taylor spoke to a mechanic on the phone, Erica scanned the office, seeming to soak it in. Taylor watched her coworker's movements and noted the pleased expression on the other woman's face. It was probably the same expression that Taylor had found on her own face the first time she realized what working for LifeLine meant. Being part of a team that helped to save lives felt good.

Concluding her conversation, she cradled the phone. The rattle prompted Erica to swing around and speak. "I guess we're done, huh?"

"Yeah, looks like it." Taylor dropped her legs off the edge of the desk and stood. "I guess we covered everything we needed tonight. I'll go ahead and sign you off and tell Nate he can put you on the schedule." She zipped her brown leather flight jacket and opened the door to the parking lot. Standing in the doorway, she gestured at the schedule board hanging behind her. "Of course, you'll get night shift when you start, that's the one everybody hates. Four p.m. to four a.m. Newcomers get all the crummy duty time for a while, but I wouldn't worry. It'll change every two weeks." She stepped into the asphalt parking square, empty but for her car and Erica's. "I'll see you tomorrow, then. Or is it tomorrow already?" She glanced at her watch, then shrugged when she saw it wasn't quite midnight yet.

"So," Erica asked, "you want to go get a Coke or something? I'm still kinda wired, maybe something to drink will quiet me down."

"Yeah, I guess we can go get something, I'm not on duty tonight. Sounds like a plan."

Taylor was looking forward to getting to know Erica. Most of her friends were pilots, which meant most of her friends were male. A woman would be a nice change.

After all, she couldn't take any of her male friends on a trip downtown to Nordstrom to shop for underwear.

The two women piled into Erica's aqua Geo Metro and fastened their seat belts. Taylor's eyebrows rose. "This isn't really a car, is it?" She snickered.

"Aww, don't bad-mouth my car. When I lived in Wasilla, I needed a good economical car for the commute, but now that I live closer, I still like saving money on gas." Erica snuggled into the driver's seat and asked, "Where to? Do you guys go anywhere special?"

"Yeah, we do. Head for that hotel at the intersection of International and Spenard."

On the way, she learned that Erica had gone to high school in Fairbanks, where her parents still lived; that she did a lot of reading in her spare time; and that she was separated from the husband she'd listed on her job application. "Even though we're gonna split up, I figured he should get the health insurance until then. Medical care is so expensive," Erica explained.

Nodding, she directed Erica to turn off into a parking lot near Lake Spenard. They saw a late arrival coming in for a landing at the lake, a Cessna 185 seaplane drifting down the final approach to the inky nighttime water, the white landing lights and red and green wingtip strobes flickering color across its surface.

By the time Taylor and Erica were seated at a table near

the windows, the plane was out of sight and no other activity had developed. Finally, it was dark and the only things readily identifiable were the two canals connecting Lake Spenard with its twin, Lake Hood, where blue and white globes marked the banks. Turning away from the view, Taylor scanned the nearly empty restaurant-bar area.

"Hey, there's Cam!" she acknowledged, pointing at a corner table where two men sat. "Hey, Cam! Over here!" The two men looked up, surveying the occupied tables, then identified Taylor. "That guy on the left is Cameron McNiven," she said. "He's one of the other King Air copilots."

Erica followed Taylor's gesture and nodded. "Yeah, I know him."

A surprised look flickered across Taylor's face. "You do? From where?"

"He's the one who told me about this job."

"He did?" That surprised Taylor. Nate Mueller, the office manager, hadn't mentioned that when he gave her the paperwork on the new hire. "You must know him pretty well."

"Uhhh . . ." Erica shrugged.

Taylor waved the men over. Cameron had boyish good looks framed by well-trimmed dark hair and a mustache, and the subtle hint of sagging jowls indicated that he was probably just over the age-thirty hill. The brown leather flight jacket he had swung over his shoulder was identical to the one Taylor wore, and his casual outfit had the unstudied but careful look of someone trying hard not to look as though he spent any time with his appearance.

The younger man at his side was a deep contrast—his light brown hair fell from his head in long waves and partially concealed cheeks riddled with acne scars. The goatee on his chin made him look like part of a grunge rock band, and his saunter was like a neon sign proclaiming how cool he thought he was.

As they approached the table, Erica grabbed the dessert menu and studied it.

Noticing that, Taylor teased her. "Worked up an appetite during your checkout, huh?" She laughed.

The other woman glanced up. "I'm starving," she said simply and turned back to the menu.

"Hi there, Taylor, Rickie," Cameron said upon reaching the table.

"Rickie?" Taylor squinted at her companion. "Your nickname is Rickie?"

"Well, yeah, I guess it is," she muttered.

"Hey, that's a neat nickname, can I call you that?"

With an emphatic shake of her head Erica nixed the idea. "Naw, why don't you use my full name. It sounds more professional."

"Well, okay, I don't want to tick you off," Taylor acknowledged, "but I still think it's neat."

Another shrug and a tentative smile took the place of an answer from Erica.

Appearing to ignore Erica's unease, Cameron put his arm around the shoulders of the other man in a proprietary way. "I don't think you've met this guy, Taylor. This is my little brother, Scott. He's a wrench over at Merrill Field. I guess aviation runs in our family's blood, huh?"

Extending her hand to shake Scott's, Taylor greeted him. "I didn't see Cam's car in the parking lot. He must've been with you." She scanned the younger man's almost comical way-too-cool stance and turned back to her coworker. "I wouldn't have recognized him as a brother of yours, Cam. Were you adopted, or was he?"

After a polite laugh from Cameron, she nodded at Erica. "She got her King Air checkout tonight, and I think it wore her out. We had a gear problem. They wouldn't come down and I thought we were gonna have to land gear up. But"— she beamed proudly, like a mother clapping for her child in a school play—"Erica handled things really well. Wasn't much of a problem after all."

Erica set her menu down and glanced up at Cameron. "I guess you already know how that goes, huh?" she said, then swung her head around to look for a waitress. "I gotta get something to eat, I'm gonna die. You see anybody to take my order?"

No waitress had appeared anywhere nearby and Taylor shook her head at the question. She turned back to the men. "Why don't you and Scott join us? It looks like we gotta get something to eat."

"Bad case of the munchies, huh?" Cameron joked.

"Yeah, right." Taylor grinned. "But no, that wasn't really it. Check rides make you hungry. Burns up a lot of calories." She smirked and gestured at a chair. "You guys gonna sit down?"

"No, we were just getting ready to leave." Cameron slipped into his jacket, then stepped back from the table. "See you at the office, Taylor."

Out of the corner of her eye, Taylor saw a familiar figure walk out of the men's rest room and head for where they were congregated. "Wait up, Cam," the tall man called out. He trotted over, his blond hair bouncing in time. He was a handsome man, in his mid-thirties, reminiscent of Robert Redford in a slimmer, almost anorexic frame. "You guys leaving without me?" he whined.

"I thought you'd already gone to the car, Dave," Cam replied apologetically.

Glancing at the seated women, Dave Kingsbury nodded at them. "Hey, Taylor. Haven't seen you for a while. Who's your friend?"

"Hi, Dave. This is Erica Wolverton. Erica, this is Dave Kingsbury." Introductions completed, she cocked her head and studied the blond man's expression. "I thought you moved to Oregon. Are you back from there, or didn't you go in the first place?"

Dave frowned, his features twisted. "I never went. I don't even have the money to get out of here." His mien darkened some more. "What'd Nate do, anyway, blackball me? I can't find a flying job in Anchorage to save my ass. I'm working in a fucking video store!"

"I'm sorry to hear about that, Dave, but I'm sure Nate didn't do anything to make it hard for you." Taylor attempted to show concern in her eyes, even though she really didn't feel it. "Good luck finding something. Maybe if you can get to Oregon, things'll look up. I know things are kinda tight up here right now."

"That's for sure." Dave sniffed. He stalked off, waving at Cam and Scott to follow.

Cam rolled his eyes for Taylor's benefit, then turned for the door.

With an amused look, Erica watched the men leave. "That Dave guy was kinda cute. What was he so pissed off about?"

"Aww, he used to be a Lear copilot for LifeLine, but he got fired. He thinks he can't find another pilot's job because Nate told everybody not to hire him, but that's not it. He can't get another job because he's just not a very good pilot. Especially in the Learjet." Taylor reached toward the dessert menu and raised her eyebrows. Erica passed it over. "Anyway, I have no idea how he got far enough in his flying career to get into the right seat of a Lear—or, for that matter, how he convinced Nate to hire him—but after a bunch of complaints from the captains, Nate had to let him go. Word travels fast when you get fired like that, that's why nobody'll hire him."

Scanning the dessert menu, Taylor checked the price column. Not too bad, she had enough cash to get something. "So, Erica, ready for your first medevac? Maybe in a day or two, should be fun."

"Boy, I sure am ready for some fun. Where do you think I'll have to go?"

"No way of knowing, but it could be down on the Alaska Peninsula. A lot of accidents down there during hunting season."

"Alaska Peninsula, huh? That's gorgeous country. The

Alaska Range and all of those glacier-fed lakes. Bright turquoise water. Neat.''

"Yeah, it is pretty, that's true, but you probably won't see much of it. It'll be night.'' Taylor recalled her first medevac flight onto the Alaska Peninsula. The country was beautiful, but had a dangerous side hidden by the beauty. "Remember, though, those mountains are pretty tall and rugged. Kind of hazardous at night or when you're not paying attention. There's plenty of wrecked airplanes in the passes.''

"Yeah.'' Erica nodded. "But we'll be flying IFR the whole time. No problem.''

"Well, that's right. You'll probably just have a lot of fun on that trip.'' Taylor's index finger stopped halfway down the menu and she smacked her lips. "Ah, chocolate silk pie, sounds good. Let's order. You worked me too hard on that check ride—I need to renew my energy supply.''

TWO

Three nights later, the insistent bleat of a telephone ringing pierced the stillness of the sleeping loft in Taylor Morgan's cabin. In response to the sound that always meant get-ready-for-action she bolted upright in bed and ripped the covers off her body. Her feet dropped down to a cool floor and she stood. A second later puzzlement served to halt her movement and she sat back onto the mattress with a thump.

She stared at the green LED digits on her clock radio—the lights glowered rudely at her: 4:22 a.m. Why was she getting a call for a medevac at that hour? she wondered. She wasn't on nighttime call that week, another captain was scheduled for that. And why was her phone ringing, instead of her pager beeping?

The telephone continued to clamor. Was it a wrong number? Had to be, at this hour.

She fell back on her pillow and fumbled for the receiver. "Yes?" she croaked, expecting to hear the sudden click of a hang-up.

"Taylor, wake up. It's me." When she recognized the

voice of Nate Mueller, the skin on her cheekbones retracted in surprise. She sat up again.

"Nate? What are you doing calling me this early? I'm not on duty."

"We got trouble. Meet me at the office right away."

The color drained from her face. "Trouble? What are you talking about?" she stammered. Disturbing pictures whirled through her mind as she waited for him to answer. She knew it had to be really bad news.

It was always bad news that early in the morning.

"I just got a call from the troopers. Center reported losing a King Air. It dropped off the radar screen near Mount Iliamna."

"They lost a King Air? One of our King Airs?" Instantly, she realized how stupid that question was—why would the troopers call Nate if it was someone else's King Air?

"Yeah, one of our King Airs. Two-three-two."

A knot formed in her gut. When an aircraft dropped off the radar screen, surely it had encountered a serious problem. A life-threatening problem. Usually a fatal crash.

"Nate, who was crewing two-three-two?" she murmured, hearing the tremor in her voice. A list of possibles was scrolling across her mind, and she knew she had probably lost some friends that night.

Nate coughed. "Marshall Price flying left seat, two flight nurses in back, Jocelyn Evans and Gwen Littleton." He spoke matter-of-factly, trying to disguise his emotion. "And the new hire in the right seat. The girl, Erica."

"Ohhh, Nate, not them." Taylor closed her eyes and slumped back down on the mattress. Price had been something of a role model for her when she'd started at LifeLine, and the nurses were easygoing, spirited coworkers, fun to fly with. She'd miss them desperately if they'd perished in the crash.

Then she focused on the last person Nate had mentioned: the newcomer, Erica. Even though they hadn't known each other long, she had had high hopes for the younger woman. Erica made her remember her own beginnings as a medevac pilot, and that immediately brought the two women closer in her mind.

She had given Erica a brief pep talk not nine hours earlier when a medevac had been dispatched, and the younger woman was slated to be on the crew that took the flight. She had been excited—her first duty call. The three days since her checkout had been hell for her, having to wait by patiently when medevacs were assigned to other pilots. But finally, she'd gotten her chance.

And look what had happened.

Suddenly, Taylor jerked her head up. "But it could be nothing but an equipment failure, Nate. They might have made an off-airport landing in the hills. They may be okay . . ."

But she knew better. The state troopers didn't call when the people on board were merely waiting on the ground for a helicopter pickup. Only a catastrophic accident warranted notification from the troopers.

"No, Taylor, you know they're not just sitting on the ground. They didn't call Center with an emergency, and an ELT was picked up. A Coast Guard C-130 went out to check on it, but it was too dark to see anything so they're sending a helicopter out at first light. The plane disappeared from the screen near Mount Iliamna, and I'm afraid that . . ." He stopped in mid-sentence, his composure gone. "Well, I'm not going to speculate. You're gonna have to go help locate the crash site, figure things out."

She gritted her teeth—that was grisly duty, but she wouldn't refuse it. Her friends were down there. Tucking the phone between her chin and shoulder, she reached for a pair of jeans lying in the corner. "I'll meet you at the office in about a half hour," she muttered, and cradled the phone.

Half in a daze, Taylor grabbed the rest of a pile of clothes scattered about the loft. Socks. Sneakers. A rumpled sweat-shirt.

By the time she had tumbled down the ladder from the loft and slipped her flight jacket on, she had pulled herself out of the daze but was working herself into an agitated frenzy. The same question flashed in her brain like a garish neon sign: What happened? What happened? What happened? She desperately wanted the answer to that question, though at the same time she knew the answer would devastate her.

After stepping out of the cabin into the cool early dawn air, she carefully locked the door and scanned the heavily wooded area around her. Experience had taught her to cross-check the grounds before leaving the house—several times while building her cabin, she'd seen wild animals nearby. The small ones—the squirrels, the porcupines, the foxes—were no problem, but once she'd spotted a young black bear eating berries on an adjacent hill, twenty-five feet away.

That was a bit too close for her peace of mind.

The bear had noticed her at the same time she noticed him, and she hoped she did not look any tastier than the cranberries he was snacking on. Fortunately, as Taylor beat feet for the security of a stack of lumber she heard the crackle of twigs that signaled the bear dashing in the opposite direction.

Nobody had ever accused Taylor of being a slow learner, so that single close encounter with Smokey the Bear was all it took to make her change her habits. Even though she knew that the black and brown bears known to frequent the neighboring Chugach State Park were usually as wary of humans as humans were of them, she didn't want to surprise one like that again.

Especially at midnight, when she wandered out of the cabin half-asleep, after getting a call for a medevac.

In addition, a number of moose called the adjoining woods home and could be found browsing on the ornamental shrubs she'd added to her landscaping. Moose had been known to trample humans to death when startled or when protecting their calves, so Taylor never blasted out the door without being aware of what was around her.

The wildlife was one of the reasons she loved her cabin on Anchorage's Upper Hillside. Undeveloped land surrounded the compact home, with wonderful views of mountains and spruce forests filling every window, but Anchorage's International Airport sat only twenty miles away. The best of both worlds.

Once Taylor had assured herself that no trouble existed outside, she fumbled in her pocket for the keys to her four-wheel-drive Suzuki Sidekick. One of the drawbacks of living in virtual wilderness was the roads that demanded a car like the Sidekick. The driveway from the nearest asphalt street to her cabin was two hundred feet of bad news—the rutted dirt road was mostly quagmire during the spring thaw and mostly snowdrifts during the seven months of Anchorage's winter.

A pitfall in living on the Upper Hillside was the amount of snowfall found at that higher elevation—the area around her cabin got snow earlier than the Anchorage bowl did, and got more of it. She'd spent many hours hefting a snow shovel, clearing a way from the cabin to her car, then another half an hour trying to find the car buried under a foot or two of snow.

Fortunately, Taylor had neither mud nor snow to contend with that early morning.

She clambered into the driver's seat and zoomed off toward the airport. With every jounce over a hummock in the long driveway she pounded on the steering wheel, agonizing over what had occurred only hours earlier hundreds of miles away on the Alaska Peninsula.

Once she found the better footing of the paved road at the end of the driveway, her pounding ended and she drove the Sidekick as though on autopilot. She never saw the asphalt under her wheels, she never recognized the elegant, expensive homes that peppered the streets. Her thoughts were locked on one fact—one of their aircraft had gone down with five people on board, and nobody knew why.

A multitude of questions begged for an answer.

What if they'd had an engine failure? Or if *both* engines quit?

She digested that idea, then shook her head. If disaster struck somehow, the pilots were trained to handle single and dual engine failures. Single failures were simple to deal with, as twin-engine planes were designed to fly on one if need be.

And if both quit, well, doing an emergency landing without power—a dead-stick landing—was a vital part of every pilot's education. Even though Taylor hadn't tested Erica on her ability to manage one, she was sure the new copilot could do it safely.

As she searched for the accident's cause, a disturbing idea nagged for a response. Had one of the crew members caused the crash? She hated to think of that, but pilot error was one of the first things looked into when investigating an accident.

Her grip on the steering wheel tightened when she contemplated that possibility, but she shook her head vehemently. She couldn't believe a screwup had occurred—the LifeLine pilots had experience, were well schooled.

Then she mentally backtracked.

Erica wasn't really all that expert, and she was new to the King Air. Could her lack of familiarity have been at fault in the crash? Taylor's eyes narrowed for an instant before she ground her teeth and refused to believe her coworker had been involved.

After all, Taylor had flown with her, checked her out in the King Air, and was more than satisfied with the younger woman's performance. That couldn't be it.

It had to be something else.

Lifting one hand from the steering wheel, she gnawed on a fingernail. An unlikely, but frightening, idea came to her—was it possible that the patient, crazed by drugs, had done something dangerous to the plane? Taylor could remember seeing TV movies where a person bound onto a stretcher broke free, tearing his IV needle off and going berserk in the ER. She shuddered thinking about a maddened patient wreaking havoc inside the confines of the aircraft's cabin. She didn't want to dwell on that.

After stopping at a red light on O'Malley, she turned right and accelerated up the Seward Highway on-ramp. A few cars sped by, the traffic extremely light due to the early hour. Within ninety minutes, the Seward Highway's northbound lane would be clogged with vehicles, their drivers playing combat commuting as they fought their way into downtown Anchorage.

No plausible cause for the crash had surfaced during her drive. She couldn't make any sense of what had occurred, try as she might. She certainly didn't want to give any credence to the idea that the accident had been due to a pilot's mistake. If that was true, a possibility existed that someday the same thing could happen to her.

That was a sobering thought.

She tried to prevent this distraction by strengthening her focus on the current situation. All she knew so far was that fatalities were likely—she cringed when she acknowledged the chance that *everyone* on board had been killed. Two nurses, an injured or sick person, and two pilots.

Two pilots. And one of them was Erica.

The noise of Taylor smacking the black plastic shift lever knob with the flat of her hand resonated around the Suzuki.

Even though she had just met Erica, she had already taken a liking to her. The younger woman reminded her so much of her own beginnings as a pilot, and she was really looking forward to making a friend. Surely they could have gotten close, with both of them experiencing the pitfalls that were always part of a woman's life when she worked in a career field dominated by men. Taylor's few female friends were not in aviation, so they were unable to really relate to those kind of stories.

But Erica would have.

If she was alive.

That tiny fragment of hope, that Erica had survived the crash, allowed her to make it to the LifeLine office. She wouldn't let herself acknowledge the loss of a woman who had held so much promise in her eyes. Not until they sorted through the wreckage of the King Air, and saw no traces of life, would she give up.

Arriving at the LifeLine office, she turned the ignition off and leaned against the steering wheel. She felt like she had just been beaten up. She'd never experienced *that* before when notified of a plane wreck, so why was it affecting her this time?

With a shove, she pushed away from the steering wheel. Maybe this time the tragedy was hitting a lot closer to home, she thought. Seeing another woman meet her end in an airplane crash seemed to underscore Taylor's own mortality.

The car door squeaked slightly when she pushed it open, and she stared blankly at the asphalt below. She didn't want to walk into the LifeLine office, to see the expression on Nate's face that meant disaster. Without a doubt, there would be a trooper there, too, and maybe an investigator from the National Transportation Safety Board. Plans had to be made to get out to the crash site, to search for survivors, to collect the bodies of the dead.

That wasn't her idea of fun, but she wouldn't be able to get out of it. She was the check pilot for the King Air and had been responsible for training Erica; she was the logical person to send. If there was any hint of pilot involvement in the crash, her input would be needed.

Hesitantly, she lowered her feet to the ground and sighed. Where was Steve when she needed him to lean on? Probably still sitting in Seattle with the Learjet. No telling when he'd be back. Damn.

Not only was Steve Derossett another LifeLine pilot who knew the way things ran, he might bring something to the situation, see something Taylor couldn't.

Sliding out of the Suzuki, she trudged up to the office's front door. Through the burgundy-and-silver decal on the door she could see Nate Mueller sitting stiffly upright in the chair at his desk. To his left stood two unfamiliar men, and she guessed they were troopers. When she got closer, she saw flat-brimmed hats in their hands. The door's hydraulic arm *wooshed* as she pushed into the room and marched up behind them.

"Taylor, you're here!" stuttered Nate Mueller. "What'd you do, speed? You got here pretty fast. I didn't know when to expect you. Was there any traffic?" He stood, inadvertently pushing his chair back too far, causing it to hit the schedule board behind him with a thud. He nudged his glasses farther up on his nose and ran the same hand through his dark brown hair several times. His appearance was as crumpled as hers—his denim shirt was wrinkled, his corduroy pants beltless.

His nonsensical speech and jerky movements seemed frantic. If Taylor didn't know better she'd think he was on something. The ramifications of the crash were clearly getting to him, too.

She glanced at him, then the strangers beside him quizzically. He caught the question in her eyes and gestured at the two uniformed men. "This is Trooper Hall and his partner, Sergeant Ferdin. They'll be coming with you to the crash site."

Hall looked as though he had just graduated from trooper finishing school. Tall, lean, dark, clean-shaven, and wellcreased. The name tag above his chest pocket was set just so; the gold buttons on his uniform shone. Even his shoes gleamed. His athletic frame spoke of a man who tended to his body religiously.

Ferdin seemed to be the complete opposite. Medium height, chubby, pasty complexion, disheveled, even a bit seedy-looking, despite his uniform. The only thing that matched between the two troopers was their apparent age—both men looked to be in their early forties.

She accounted for the difference in their builds by noting that Ferdin held higher rank than Hall, and he probably sat at a desk for longer hours. Hence the accompanying bulge at the midriff. She wondered how he would do at the crash site, which was ostensibly somewhere on the slopes of Mt. Iliamna, and wouldn't be an easy hike.

She snapped out of her reverie and offered a hand for either of the troopers to shake. "Trooper Hall, Sergeant Ferdin, I'm Taylor Morgan. I'll be going with you. Are we waiting for anyone else? If not, we'd better get going; there may be survivors that need help."

Before Hall or Ferdin could answer, the door from the hangar opened to allow the entry of another new face. The man's brisk pace belied the early hour; his erect posture was decidedly military. He, too, was dressed in an Alaska State Troopers uniform, and the earplug container dangling from a belt loop suggested he was the pilot for the Troopers' helicopter.

The trooper pilot approached his fellow officers and nodded in a proprietary way toward the aircraft ramp behind the building. "The ship's out back. You guys ready to go?" he said. He waved his hand at Taylor after eyeing her briefly, and asked, "This who you were waiting for? She doesn't look like an Alpine Rescue guy."

Nate interrupted quickly. "No, she's not with them, they haven't arrived yet. She's one of our people, a King Air captain. I wanted her to go with you, figure out what happened."

The pilot acknowledged Nate's comment with a bob of his head, then turned back to the other troopers. "The Coast Guard helicopter is probably in the air by now, on its way to the crash site. I'll be in contact with them once we lift off. They'll report in if they find any survivors." He cleared his throat nervously. "Doesn't sound good, though. They

located the ELT signal about five thousand feet from the
top of Mount Iliamna.''

Taylor felt her face blanch at the same time she saw Nate
turn white.

THREE

Taylor's head lolled to the side and struck the helicopter's cabin wall—the impact jerked her out of her fitful doze and her eyes snapped open.

Briefly confused by her surroundings, she started, then relaxed when she heard the *wocketa-wocketa-wocketa* of rotor blades and remembered where she was and why she was there.

She glanced about the cramped confines of the troopers' Bell Long Ranger helicopter, curious to see if anyone but she had fallen asleep. Her scan revealed that no one else had succumbed to inertia and she felt a bit embarrassed.

Sergeant Ferdin leaned forward over the backs of the two front cockpit seats, trying to be included in the conversation between Trooper Hall and the pilot. Across from him sat Tom, one of the Alpine Rescue Group members. Both he and his companion Greg, who sat opposite Taylor on the helicopter's rear bench seat, were staring out the window, entranced. Their heads framed the savage-looking blue-and-white faces on the mountains of the eastern Alaska Range.

The line of peaks stabbed into the atmosphere for two hundred and fifty miles, from the 10,016-foot Mt. Iliamna, their eventual destination, to the massive 20,320-foot Mt. McKinley. Even at the end of summer, the promontories displayed full heads of snow—the air temperature at their apexes, tens of thousands of feet above sea level, was brutally cold.

Taylor shook her head when she realized that everyone was occupied and awake. What had happened to her? After all, this was an important flight, they were on their way to a site of tragedy involving her coworkers. How could she catnap in the middle of that? Shouldn't she be busy worrying about what they were going to find when they reached Mt. Iliamna?

Clearing her throat, she prepared to engage the two Alpine Rescue men in conversation. If they saw her awake, maybe they'd think she had just been in deep thought earlier.

"You guys ever climbed any of those mountains?" she asked, her finger aimed at the nearest peak. Greg, startled by the sound of her voice, swiveled from the window.

Greg was the shorter of the two Alpine Rescue members, but only just barely. Both he and Tom were compact and sturdy—five foot eight or nine, muscular, broad shoulders, no extra flesh around their middles. She wondered if that kind of build was standard for mountain rescue workers—perhaps having a lower-than-normal center of gravity helped while maneuvering on the slopes.

The flushed cheeks on Greg's face were probably a sign of those activities, too, she thought. Windburn from time spent at high altitudes. Then she remembered that winter hadn't come yet—he couldn't have been involved in any mountain rescues, snatching errant cross-country skiers and snowmachine drivers off the snowy peaks near Anchorage. He must have overdone a day at the Goose Lake beach.

When he saw her pointing at the mountains outside, he shook his head. "Naw, I haven't climbed any of *these* hills," he said as he rubbed the stubble on a reddened cheek. "I've flown into the Alaska Range before, but not to climb. I was sheep hunting. Hey, Tom''—he poked his partner to catch his attention—''do you remember bagging that Dall ram last fall? I nearly killed myself getting him.''

Without taking his eyes from the surrounding mountains, Tom nodded and fingered his charcoal handlebar mustache. Even though he and Greg looked like a matched set physically, their coloring set them apart—his dark complexion and sable hair spoke of Eastern European descent, whereas the other man's golden-boy looks were pure Nordic. ''Yeah, if I hadn't caught you when you tripped, you'd've caught the pointy end of that sheep rack between your—''

''No gory details,'' Greg interrupted. He blushed furiously, his cheeks flaring a red two shades brighter than before. ''Taylor doesn't need to hear about that.''

She arched her eyebrows and smiled tentatively. ''I'm sure that's a fascinating story, guys, and I'd love to hear it, but I have a couple questions first.'' She nodded at the window. ''What can you tell me about where we're headed? I've flown past Iliamna before, but not close enough to see much. Will the pilot have a hard time finding a flat square for landing the helicopter? And—'' She paused.

Greg raised his eyebrows. ''And?'' he prodded.

''And what about the crash site, what's going to be around it? Somebody must've thought it'd be on pretty tough terrain, or they wouldn't've sent you guys along.'' She bit her lip and stopped talking as an image flashed across her mind's eye—the wrecked King Air lay crumpled, looking like a huge pile of recycled aluminum. Not a pretty picture.

Appearing to notice her discomfort, Tom spoke up quickly to fill the void. ''I got a quick briefing before we left, got some idea of what we'll be looking at. The most unusual thing, of course, is that Iliamna is a volcano—''

''A volcano?'' Taylor squeaked. ''Is it active?'' All she'd been concerned about was the crash site being on a mountainside. It never occurred to her that it was on the side of a volcano.

Alaska had many volcanoes, some active, some dormant, as part of the Pacific Ocean's Ring of Fire that stretched from California to Japan. She hoped Mt. Iliamna was dormant, unlike the nearby Mt. Redoubt that had erupted several years earlier, suffocating Southcentral Alaska with gritty, corrosive ash.

Tom laughed at her obvious anxiety. "Well, it's not really an active volcano. It steams a lot, and people are calling the Volcano Observatory all the time to says it's gonna blow, but it hasn't erupted since the 1700s." He reached down and touched the coiled ropes and duffel bag near his feet. Metal made a jangling sound as he repositioned the duffel. "But there's a bunch of glaciers around the volcano's vent—that's why we brought all of this ice climbing stuff."

"Hmmm. You think there'll be some glaciers farther down, around the crash site? That'll make getting to the airplane a lot tougher." She stopped to ponder that, then glanced out the window when another concern was triggered. She peered at the ground below the droning helicopter, then back up to meet the looks of the two men. "Where's the tree line down here? That could make a real difference in surviving the crash. If the plane hit the trees rather than the rocks, the trees would cushion the impact. . . ."

"Yeah, it would." A nod confirmed Tom's agreement. "The guy I talked to said the tree line down here is a little higher than around Anchorage, and the terrain above the tree line is different, too. Not just glaciers, but lava rock and ash from about three thousand feet up. . . ." He looked pointedly at the climbing equipment stashed underneath his seat as though reassured by its presence that he could handle the unusual facets of this mountain.

Caught up in conjecture, she dropped her head against the seat cushion. "I bet the King Air hit somewhere on the lava rock, that might not be too bad a place to crash. That means that maybe somebody survived the crash. . . .'' The faint glimmer of hope she had been nursing swelled slightly. She lurched forward and peered out a nearby window, cupping her hands around her eyes to shade them from the bright sun. ''How close to Iliamna are we now? If it's not too far off, maybe we can ask the pilot to—''

Out of the corner of her eye, she saw the pilot hold his hand up to press his radio headset tighter against his ear. She swung around to stare at him. She saw his lips move intermittently, but she couldn't hear what he said over the racket of the helicopter's rotor blades.

''Is that the Coast Guard? You getting some news from their helicopter?'' Her voice cracked in her effort to be heard above the din.

When the man's hand dropped from his headset and he swiveled to look at her, the message in his eyes answered her question. Her gut contracted, feeling like it was rising up her abdomen, choking her. ''What?'' she yelled over the clattering blades. ''What? What'd they say?''

The pilot set his jaw, then leaned over his seat back to get closer. ''The Coast Guard chopper is back at its base,'' he said, his words clipped. ''They checked the crash site.'' He paused, and shook his head. ''No survivors.''

Shaken, Taylor gaped at the pilot. ''No survivors? Are they sure?'' The timbre of her voice raised an octave. She wanted to deny what she'd just heard.

''Yeah, they're sure. There wasn't much of anything left.''

She could feel the blood drain from her face, and she bent forward, cradling her head in her hands. ''Ohhhh . . .'' she groaned. She'd never dealt with an airplane crash involving coworkers—it was a wrenching feeling. She had continued to hold on to hope, even in the light of slim odds, but now it was useless to do so. The pilots were gone, the flight nurses were gone, even the nameless patient was gone. It hurt to be so close to tragedy like that.

She leaned back and closed her eyes.

The next ten minutes passed by without her acknowledgment, as she focused on thoughts of the friends she had lost, and how they had died. She didn't want to talk to anyone, didn't even want to keep track of the helicopter's progress. What did it matter, then? Regardless of how quickly they reached the crash site, no one would be waiting anxiously for them, anticipating an airlift to the nearest hospital.

She felt numb.

When Greg tugged on her seat belt minutes later, she opened her eyes. "Is this snugged down?" he asked, pulling on the webbing before gesturing at the terrain outside. "We're getting ready to set down—it might be a little rough."

She tightened her belt and peered out the window. The entire Alaska Range sprawled across the horizon—craggy mountaintops surrounded them, everywhere they looked. Peaks lower than Iliamna sat to the southwest; those taller peered over them from the northeast. In the distance Mt. McKinley glistened in the bright daylight, massive and formidable—more than two hundred and fifty miles away, it still looked enormous.

Farther down the slope of the volcano she could see the tree line, where the stunted spruce trees became sparse and the alpine vegetation started. Eventually, even the stubby weed-like growths that favored higher altitudes gave way to lava rock and ash deposits. The blue-white fingers of a river of ice splayed out ahead of them, about a quarter mile away. She shuddered, anxiously hoping the King Air hadn't found its final resting place on one of the glaciers. That would further complicate the retrieval of the bodies and the investigation of the crash.

The *whop-whop-whop* of the rotor blades began to bleed off as the trooper pilot slowed the helicopter. As he lowered it toward the ground, the patches of snow remaining from the past winter blustered about, blocking the passengers' view of the mountain.

The pilot seemed to be feeling his way down, only allowing the helicopter to descend an inch at a time. It rolled slightly as he hovered it, its skids grinding on the rocks as he searched for sturdy footing.

Finally, he let it sink to the ground. After a minute or two, he shut the engine down and gestured for everyone to disembark.

Taylor was the first one to jump out, and she stood with one hand on the door, scanning the horizon. The air around her was cool and clean; a light breeze ruffled her bangs. Flat shadows mottled the slope where the morning sunlight struck nearby boulders.

"Where's the airplane?" Taylor yelled, apprehension tingeing her voice. She ran to the front of the helicopter, nearly stumbling on the scabrous terrain. Knurled hummocks of lava rock covered the ground; the landing patch looked like it belonged on the surface of the moon. Nervously, she leaned around the helicopter's nose. "I don't see the King Air! I thought we were at the crash site, where is it?" She stared at the pilot, waiting for an answer, afraid that the absence of wreckage meant the aircraft had been entirely demolished and was nothing but tiny fragments littering the hill.

"It's on the other side of the ridge," said the pilot, pointing to his right. "This was the closest I could get. The plane's about half a mile away." His gesture encompassed the lava rock that formed gullies and protrusions on the hillside.

When she noted the steepness of the slope, she realized that getting to the crash site would be difficult. "Damn," she whispered.

The Alpine Rescue men had already studied the ridge and were rummaging through their duffel bags. "Won't take us too long to get over there," Tom said, turning toward the troopers. "We'll start bringing the bodies down. You guys have the bags?"

"Wait a minute, we're coming with you," Hall replied. "It doesn't look too bad; we can handle it."

Ferdin surveyed the slope ahead doubtfully. Taylor could tell that he wished his partner hadn't volunteered them to accompany the climbers—perhaps he had hoped the crash site was on a glacier so that he wouldn't have to go.

"Hey, there's no way I'm going to stay here, either," Taylor insisted. "If the troopers are going, I'm going, too. Those are my friends over there. I have to find out what happened." She strode over to Tom and grabbed up one of the coils of rope. Tugging on the loose end, she looked up at him expectantly. "Show me how this goes. Do I need a harness, or what?"

FOUR

Fifteen minutes later Taylor Morgan stood on the top of the ridge, staring down the slope on the far side. Her chest rose and fell as she gulped at the thin air. She could feel blood dribbling down her pants leg from a gash on her knee, and abrasions on the heel of her right hand throbbed rhythmically. Her jeans, not too clean to start with, had dark smudges and stains on them from scrambling over rocks and boulders.

But even her disheveled appearance could not match the grim look on her face.

One hundred feet downslope from where she stood, at a point where glaciated ice met black lava rock, lay the fuselage of the King Air, looking like a giant can opener had carved it into pieces. Medical supplies from inside the cabin lay strewn across the rough terrain, dots of sterile white on ashen black.

The only intact piece of the aircraft was the vertical tail, which stood away from the rest of the wreckage like a man-height capital "T." She turned away from the sight of the burgundy-and-silver logo at its base—it reminded her of the markings on a gravestone.

She hadn't ever been so close to a crash site. Most of the time she only heard the grisly anecdotes about fatal plane wrecks, but she rarely saw the wreckage itself, and then only in photos. But this time, not only could she see the aftermath of an accident, she knew who was hidden in the heap of charred aluminum on the ground.

Behind her, she heard grunts and groans as Greg helped Trooper Hall and a struggling Sergeant Ferdin to the top of the ridge. The sounds of labored breathing reached her from nearby, as well—Tom was panting, too, though fatigue didn't seem to be the entire cause of his gasps. He stared goggle-eyed at the mangled aluminum mess below him. "Damn. That looks like bad news," he muttered, touching her elbow to lead her downhill.

Her face contorted briefly—she didn't want to examine the scarred metal sarcophagus holding the remains of her coworkers—but she forced herself to look more stoic. She wasn't about to show that the situation had gotten to her— that was too fragile, too weak, and she had to appear strong.

Ever since she had entered the male-dominated field of aviation she found herself stifling any signs of emotion. She didn't know if it was necessary or not, but she felt displaying any feelings made her seem unfit to work in the rough-and-tumble world of flying on the Last Frontier. She confined any show of a feminine side to private moments, and even then it was difficult to shift into a more emotive state.

Tom noted her resolute expression, then removed his hand from her arm and started down the hill.

She joined him moments later, carefully navigating the rolling humps of lava rock. The nearby crackle of dislodged gravel startled her, and she looked over her shoulder to see the tall trooper floundering toward her. "Any idea what happened down there?" he asked matter-of-factly.

His coolness surprised her for a moment, then she figured it out. Certainly, he had seen many fatal crashes in the past, and this one wasn't any different. She wondered if he'd ever gone to an accident scene where *he'd* known the victims—did it ever get any easier, controlling your emotions in a situation like that?

Turning away from the trooper, she continued picking her way down the hill. "No way of telling until we get there," she called back to him. As she stepped past one of the many patches of snow dotting the slope, she glanced at the torn, bloodstained denim near her right knee. She felt as though she deserved her injuries—there she was, alive, while her coworkers lay dead only yards away. They had paid the ultimate price for their love of aviation; her nicks and cuts were no match for that.

When she reached the remains of the aircraft, she averted her eyes, unsure of how she would handle getting a closer look at the carnage inside. She was glad that no breakfast or lunch weighed her stomach down; she certainly would have lost it.

That would look real good.

When Hall reached her side she finally raised her head and forced herself to peer into the gaping crack between the cockpit and the aircraft's cabin. "Oh, good Lord." She breathed heavily as they scanned the chaos in front of them. She'd expected damage, but it still shocked her.

The bench holding the patient had wrenched away from the cabin wall, ejecting the male Alaskan native on top of flight nurse Jocelyn Evans. In one hand she held the pressurized IV bag connected to the man, with the other she appeared to be pushing him back from her tense body. All of the loose medical supplies in the cabin had been impelled to the front, and a handheld oxygen delivery system dangled out the ragged gap in the fuselage.

The bulkhead wall that separated the pilots from the passengers was in splinters, partially collapsed over the bodies in the cockpit. Only one of the windows had survived the crash, the others were cracked and crazed, or gone entirely. The aircraft's captain, Marshall Price, sat trapped in his seat, his shoulder harness pinning him in place behind the mangled metal of the control yoke. An oxygen mask was clipped to his face.

In the narrow space between the two pilot's seats sprawled the body of Gwen Littleton, the second flight nurse. One of her hands still gripped the captain's control yoke as though to steady herself.

As Taylor surveyed the bodies in the cockpit, then stooped to study Erica, her gaze narrowed. "This isn't right," she mumbled, and attempted to clamber through the rough split torn through the aircraft's fuselage.

"Where are you going?" demanded Hall. "We'll get the bodies out—don't touch them."

"But there's something wrong here, I gotta get in." She grunted as she pulled herself past the aluminum shards. Her unease about looking closely at the bodies disappeared; all she saw was a riddle.

With her head and half of her body inside the cockpit, she squinted at the inert copilot. She was slung over her own control yoke, her head lolling at an odd angle.

Taylor made a tiny strangled noise. "Oh, damn . . ." she mewled, staring at Erica with pity in her eyes before lowering her gaze. She had to get control of herself.

Several seconds passed before she could steady her emotions, but once she could raise her head, she focused on Erica's face and peered at her intently.

A frown wrinkled Taylor's forehead. "Why doesn't she have her mask on?" she questioned rhetorically, her eyes darting back to lock on Marshall Price before returning.

"What do you mean, where's her mask? You mean an oxygen mask?" asked Hall, who had found an entrance into the aircraft from the opposite side and was working his way into the torn cockpit. "Why would she need a mask on?"

"I don't know, but he's got *his* on." She pointed at the aircraft's captain. "If there was a reason for him to put his mask on, *she* would've done the same thing. Doesn't make sense that she hadn't." Taylor pulled herself farther into the cockpit, then yelped as she fell in, headfirst. "Oh, damn!'' she cursed as she struggled to extract herself.

The trooper had pulled himself through the opposite entrance, and Taylor caught his fixed gaze. He stared at the body of Gwen Littleton, wedged in next to the captain's. ''They must've hit pretty hard for her to get thrown all the way up into the cockpit from the cabin. That would take a lot of force.''

''Yeah, it would,'' she agreed, ''but I don't think they hit as hard as you think. If they'd hit that hard, this entire aircraft would've disintegrated. There'd be nothing here, not even bodies. Just squares of metal and flesh covering the hillside.'' Her eyes focused on Gwen's hand locked on Marshall's control yoke. ''But if she didn't get thrown up here, she must've had some other reason to come forward.''

Hall absently scanned the cockpit, then snapped his fingers. ''I got it! The oxygen mask he's wearing, the one you wondered about? Maybe Price was having a heart attack or a stroke, and she came up to put the mask on him. That'd make sense, wouldn't it? He'd need oxygen if he was in trouble—''

''Naw, I don't think that's it,'' she demurred. ''Good guess, but . . . Even if Marshall was having a heart attack, that doesn't explain why they crashed. Erica could've handled the ship by herself, she didn't need him.''

''Well, maybe they had some kind of mechanical problem, too, one she couldn't take care of. Things got away from her, she panicked.''

Taylor glared at him. The assumption that a woman couldn't face aircraft problems without losing her cool didn't sit well with her. The ''weak, hysterical female'' theory wasn't going to cut it. ''Oh, come on, Hall, what kind of coincidence would that be? Marshall has a heart attack at the exact same time that something goes to shit with the airplane? Give me a break!''

''It might not have been coincidence, one might've triggered the other. Say there was a major malfunction with the plane, and Price gets so worked up trying to fix it that he has a heart attack. That could happen, couldn't it?''

"No, I don't think so. I can't believe that Marshall would lose it like that, he knows the ship too well. Plus, if anything that bad happened, Erica'd make an emergency call to Center, tell them that they were in trouble. But nobody heard anything, there was no call.'' She glanced around the wreckage, a frown contorting her face. "There's nothing here that points to a failure, nothing I can see.''

"Hey, that's just it. It could've been an engine problem—you wouldn't see that from in here. I'm sure there's a bunch of things that could've gone wrong that you couldn't see.''

"Yeah, maybe . . .'' She pushed herself toward the opening Hall had come in. She realized that what he'd said could be true, though she had a hard time acknowledging it. Dragging herself through the gaping hole in the fuselage, she grudgingly agreed with him. "You might have a point, Officer. I'll poke around outside, see if anything catches my eye.'' She stepped outside onto the rough ground.

Next to the plane's fuselage, Tom and Greg were helping Sergeant Ferdin zip the unnamed medevac patient into a body bag. The stiff form of Jocelyn Evans had been dragged out of the aircraft's cabin, too, and occupied a flat spot on the lava rock.

The flight nurse hadn't been placed in a body bag yet. Taylor glanced at the corpse, but one glimpse of a hank of blond hair lying across a pair of sightless blue eyes was all she could take. She swallowed the mouthful of bile that surged from her gut, and aimed her eyes at the aircraft as she walked past Jocelyn. Trudging along the fuselage, she touched the mangled shards of aluminum, examining them for something, anything, that looked out of place.

Above her, she heard the faint ululation of an eagle, and she stared skyward to follow the flight of his golden body. He swept past, his eyes never dipping to study the scene below as he rode an air current upwards. Whatever he thought of humans and their tawdry affairs, they didn't bother him.

When she reached the aircraft's forward wing root she veered to her right and walked down the leading edge toward the engine. Of course, the power plant would be a likely source for a malfunction, *if* there had been a malfunction. However, she was not a mechanic and that would hamper her efforts to locate any trouble spots. Still, she peered inside the engine cowling, thinking that she would notice if anything obvious was amiss.

She scanned the Pratt and Whitney PT-6, from end to end, forward to aft, without any success. She shrugged—most likely there wasn't anything wrong with the engine. Even if some malfunction resulted in the crash, it would be up to the National Transportation Safety Board technicians to examine the aircraft's systems. They had the equipment to do that, she didn't.

In the name of thoroughness, she decided to check the other power plant, just in case. That would give her something to do, something other than help with the removal of the bodies. She set to occupying herself, knowing she might lose it if she had to pull Erica from the cockpit.

She'd had such high hopes for her budding friendship with Erica. In her fantasy, she and the other woman had become fast friends, flying together, supporting each other. But the reality was seeing her body, crushed inside the King Air, and that weighed heavily on her.

On her way toward the number two engine, she walked past the rear section of the cabin, where the airstair door attached to the fuselage. That piece of structure had been altered for the medevac version of the King Air—the standard airstair door was merely the center segment of a larger hatch, one wide enough to permit the loading of a patient and a stretcher.

The impact of the aircraft hitting the side of the volcano stripped the modified door from the body, and it slumped on the ground near the wreckage on a patch of dirty snow. She glanced at it as she plodded past, then stopped and took a second look.

Something was wrong.

The smaller part of the airstair had broken away from the larger panel, but that didn't make sense. If the strength of the crash had torn the larger door from the aircraft, the smaller part would have gone with it, too, still attached.

But it had disconnected.

She bent over and scanned the heavy metal piece. Reaching down, she eyed all of the six thick bolts that coupled the two sections to each other.

Immediately, she understood the story the inanimate objects told: hacksaw grooves riddled the sides of the bolts, showing the marks of an attempt to weaken them. When a strong shearing force occurred—like when the aircraft slammed into the mountain—the crippled bolts gave way, and the smaller door segment detached from the larger one, just as the larger one tore free of the body of the plane.

Rocking back on her heels, she pondered what she'd found. Yes, someone had taken a hacksaw to the airstair's connective bolts, but why?

If any part of the door came off the plane as a result of a crash, it wouldn't really matter in the long run. The torn door would be secondary to the major damage done when the airplane hit the mountain. Why even fuss with smaller parts themselves?

As she studied the doctored bolts, Officer Hall yelled from the front of the aircraft. "Hey, Taylor! We're almost ready to start back to the helicopter! Finish up there, okay?"

"All right, I'm all done." She grunted as she stood, her knees creaking. The gash on her leg began to throb again when she moved. She must be getting old, she thought, she didn't heal as quickly as she used to. If that was how thirty-five felt, she wasn't looking forward to fifty.

During her walk toward the rest of the group, she contemplated telling someone about her discovery, then decided against it. They wouldn't really understand what she'd found. Anyway, she might be exaggerating the importance of the riddle she had stumbled upon—if it meant anything, the NTSB would note it when they came out to investigate the accident.

When she swung around the nose of the King Air, she caught herself in mid-stride. The forms of Erica Wolverton, Gwen Littleton, and Marshall Price lay directly in front of her. All three had been extracted from the cockpit, but none of them had been zipped into body bags.

She felt herself blanch. An odd sensation rushed through her gut when she steeled herself to look down at Erica. It was gruesome, seeing the other woman's blond curls matted to her head by dried blood. She wanted to turn away, but forced herself to look at the copilot's limp form in a lame attempt to say good-bye to her.

She let her eyes travel across the inert body slowly, then halted at the other woman's face. She lingered there, and a second passed before she felt her eyes widen in surprise. Jerking around, she looked at the other two corpses.

Gwen still lay exposed, but the troopers were lifting Marshall Price into a body bag. "Hey, wait a second," she called out to Hall, who was reaching to zip Price into the enclosure. "I gotta look at him!"

The lean officer looked up, surprised. "Why would you want to do that?" he asked, apparently confused by her morbid curiosity.

"Just give me a sec," she insisted. Pulling the bag open, she concentrated on the captain's face, then swung back to compare it to his copilot's. "It's the same as hers," she muttered. "Both of them are like that."

"What are you talking about, what's wrong with them?" Hall knelt down to look at the dead man more closely, a question in his eyes. He gestured to his partner.

Pointing at Erica, then at Marshall, Taylor attempted to attract the troopers' attention to the still faces. "Look at them, they're both the same color. Vivid red. Isn't that kinda weird? They look like a couple of lobsters. Why would that've happened?"

Hall's anxious expression bled away. "That's all you were worried about?" he growled. "That's not abnormal. That's called postmortem lividity; it happens all the time." He bent to finish zipping the bag.

"Postmortem lividity?" Taylor looked from him to Ferdin, then back, waiting for an explanation. "What's that mean?"

The sergeant glanced at her, then looked over to where Tom and Greg were beginning to ascend the ridge again. Over his shoulder, he said, "That's where the blood pools at the lowest part of the body after death. Pretty typical." He started heading toward the climbers. "They must be going to get the slings, Hall. I'm going to go help."

The chubby trooper's decision to scale the ridge again surprised her. If he was that eager to exert some more energy by climbing the slope, he must be pretty uncomfortable about handling the bodies. She sniffed. She wasn't too keen on helping Hall put the bodies in the bags, either, but these were her friends. It wasn't like death was contagious or anything.

She bent to pick up Erica's feet, then froze. Her second look at the other woman's cherry-red face made her compare it to Gwen's pallor. Standing abruptly, she quizzed Hall. "This is postmortem lividity? I have a hard time believing that."

He looked down at the body, then up to Taylor with his arms akimbo, seemingly annoyed by the question of his experience. "What do you mean, you don't believe it? Makes sense to me. That lividity happens more often than not in fatal accidents. How many wrecks have you covered?"

She shrugged. "None, but I still know how to think. The other trooper said 'blood pools at the lowest point' and Erica and Marshall were sitting up when we found them. That would make the lowest point somewhere below their waists. But look at her." She pointed at the lifeless copilot.

"She's red from the top of her head all the way down. Even her hands are red. Plus, check out Gwen, she's as colorless as an albino. The pilots are red, Gwen's white. I suspect the others are white, too."

He answered distractedly, after glancing at the bodies. "Yeah, I guess they are white."

"What else could that mean? You have any idea?"

The tall man looked up. "Hey, the medical examiner makes those calls. I just retrieve the bodies." He peered up the slope, where the others neared the top of the ridge. Ferdin was stumbling as he dragged himself up to catch the Alpine Rescue members. Hall turned back toward Taylor. "Anyway, can you give me a hand?"

He eased his arms under Erica's shoulders, and Taylor bent to hoist her legs. She figured he didn't think her question was worth pursuing, so she let it drop for the moment.

She expected to strain to get Erica into the body bag, but the corpse was surprisingly light. Does a person weigh less once its soul has issued after death? she wondered. She tucked that thought into a back recess of her head, and turned back to her task.

Once they had Erica secured inside the body bag, she reached down to close the flaps. "Is there any way you can check on the origin of that redness?" she said, glancing up at the officer as she pulled the zipper up. "I'm kinda curious, and I'm sure you troopers have a lot of resources for figuring things like that out. Maybe you can ask the crime lab or something."

Hall shrugged—his face said he was just humoring her. "Well, one of us has to go to the autopsies for these people, that's part of our job. Ferdin hates going to autopsies, so I'll probably go myself. I can ask then, get back to you."

"Thanks." She glanced up the ridge, and saw Tom lowering a sling into the waiting arms of Greg. Ferdin was nowhere to be seen; she figured he had stayed with the pilot on the other side of the hill. "Well, looks like they're ready to start slinging these bodies to the other side. I'd better make myself useful.''

With an audible sigh, she plodded to the body bag nearest to the hill, and gestured for Greg to bring the sling.

FIVE

Taylor walked down the narrow asphalt shoulder of West International Airport Road, her knee throbbing with every step. The ache was a constant reminder of the morning's upsetting activities, and she could do without it. A slight breeze ruffled her hair: it was the ground-based twin of the stronger wind that had rattled the commuter plane she'd ridden back to Anchorage from the small town of Homer. Glancing at the Chugach Mountains to the east of town, she recognized lenticular clouds above their peaks—no wonder the ride from Homer to Anchorage had been bumpy, she thought; the lens-shaped formations meant gusts at the higher altitudes. If she'd owned a sailplane, it would have been a wonderful day to do some soaring.

Small flecks of light flashed at her from the foothills, reflections of the evening sun still fairly high on the western horizon. She surveyed the display, idly trying to decide which of the bright dots came from her cabin—it could be any one of hundreds.

The thought of her cabin made her long to be home, napping or listening to a CD on the stereo. She needed some comforting, commonplace activities like that to slow her down—she still felt wired from the morning. From that earlier-than-normal start, things had gotten progressively worse, and she yearned to forget the entire day. The *whop-whop-whop* of the helicopter's rotor blades still rang in her ears, even hours later.

She had never imagined her role as a check pilot could lead to something as disturbing as what she'd experienced earlier. The end of life was something she'd witnessed occasionally on the air ambulance, but no one close to *her* had ever died. How could the love of her life, aviation, be the purveyor of death as well? Would she perish in an airplane crash, too?

As she plodded past the airline catering services that lined the south side of International, subtle odors wafted through the cooling evening air. Roasting chickens, spices, grilling seafood. She sniffed appreciatively and her stomach growled, even though she wasn't a big fan of airline cuisine. However, the smells coming from the kitchens were tempting, surely due to the fact that it was 7:30 p.m. and she hadn't eaten anything that day.

The air cargo offices—Federal Express, UPS, even Delta and Alaska Airlines—were the only ones open that late. A few cars were parked in their lots, and a van (in desperate need of a washing) was backing up to Delta's loading dock. As she scanned the north side of International, she heard a diesel rumble on the roadway nearby. A Gray Line tour bus sped by, most likely headed for the departure ramp at the airport. Most of the vacationers on board were anticipating their flights back home, perhaps to Des Moines or maybe Cincinnati. She envied them their return to their relaxed, status quo lives, after a successful adventure in Alaska.

As she turned off International, into the LifeLine parking lot, she spied her Suzuki standing solemnly next to Erica's aqua Geo. She halted, feeling dejected as she stared at the small vehicle, then resumed her walk.

When she reached the door sporting the burgundy-and-silver LifeLine decal, she dipped her hand into her front jeans pocket for her key. She applied it to the knob, and was surprised when it turned easily. The door was open. No lights shone inside, and Nate wasn't at his desk, so she reckoned someone else had come in earlier and gone straight to the hangar.

It appeared Nate had left for the day without waiting for her return—after all, he had no idea when she'd get back. Undoubtedly, a message waited for her at home asking her to call him later. She stepped into the room, with the door swishing closed behind her.

The office lent the first dose of normalcy to her day, even though Nate's desk had been straightened up and that was unusual. Typically it appeared rather windblown, papers scattered about it, writing instruments haphazardly tossed on the doodle-strewn blotter, but that evening it looked organized. He must have needed something banal to do to distract himself from what he knew was going on hundreds of miles away.

As her eyes swung over the desk, they landed on the white enamel scheduling board behind his high-back chair. The pilot roster, holding all the names of the flight crew members, had a different look to it.

After a second she recognized what had been changed: the names of Marshall Price and Erica Wolverton had been weeded from the list. Not just erased, the entire roster had been compacted after their removal.

She stared at the board in disbelief. How could Nate be so callous? They hadn't even been dead for twenty-four hours!

Then she slowly lowered herself down onto the wooden chair in front of his desk, realizing she would have done the same thing he did. The news of the deaths would have reached him that afternoon, and he certainly didn't want a reminder of what had happened every time he looked at the scheduling board.

She didn't either, for that matter.

As she sat in the dusky, unlit office, a noise startled

her—the door from the hangar to the locker room had just squeaked open and thudded closed. Seconds later, one of the lockers clanged open. Curious, she rose from her seat and crossed the room to poke her head in the locker room.

"Cam!" she piped upon recognizing the form at one of the lockers. "I didn't know you were here!"

"Hey, Taylor, how you doing?" Cameron McNiven turned from the locker, studying her. "I heard you went down to Iliamna today with the troopers. Are you okay?"

"Well, I guess I'm all right, considering . . ." She knew she'd probably have nightmares that night, but she didn't want to let him know about that. That didn't fit her image.

"I didn't hear a helicopter out on the ramp," he said. "Where'd the troopers drop you off?"

"Actually, they dropped me off in Homer." When she saw the inquisitive expression on his face, she offered more. "The helicopter couldn't carry five passengers and five bodies at the same time, so they radioed their Anchorage headquarters and asked to have their Cheyenne meet them in Homer. The helicopter was going to ferry the bodies from Iliamna to Homer, the Cheyenne would haul them back to Anchorage. But first they had to drop me and the Alpine Rescue guys off in Homer so we could catch the next commuter flight to town. I just walked in—I had to hike over from the terminal."

"You should've called—I would've given you a ride over." He pulled his brown leather flight jacket from the locker and shrugged it on.

"It's only a quarter mile walk, no biggie. Anyway, what are you doing here this late, just got back from a flight?" She peered around his shoulder to determine if the other King Air was in the hangar. "I didn't think you were on nights this week."

"Naw, I'm not. Nate asked me to go down to Seattle with Terry Pitts to pick up another King Air. He located one to lease, we gotta go get it." He reached down and clipped the hasps on his flight case, then dragged it out of his locker. He rummaged around the locker after that, satisfying himself that he hadn't forgotten anything.

She was a bit taken aback by his lack of interest in her day at the crash site—wasn't he curious about what had happened? Then she shrugged—maybe he was just waiting for the NTSB report. She might have done that, too, if she hadn't been involved in the crash investigation from the start.

But she wanted to talk to somebody about it, even though she couldn't come right out and say so. She approached the subject in a roundabout way. "I guess nobody's heard about two-three-two going down yet, huh? I suspect it'll probably be on the late news tonight."

"Oh, they've heard about it already. I ate lunch across the street this noon, and everyone had questions for me."

"Questions, huh? What'd you say?" She was sure everyone had an opinion about the crash, and she was also sure that most of the opinions were wrong, or based on rumors.

"Well, you know how the guys are . . ." He looked uncomfortable and fiddled with his zipper.

"What do you mean, you know how the guys are?"

"As soon as they found out that a woman was part of the crew, they figured she had something to do with the crash. But you know, they're just speculating. That was the first thing they could grab on to."

She glared at him, as though it was his fault that people had jumped to that conclusion. "But you knew Erica, you know that she wouldn't screw up like that! I can't believe those jerks would say that! Fucking morons!" She slumped down on the bench and leaned against the closest locker, a scowl on her face. From the military jet jocks to the local air taxi pilots, she'd often run into the assumption that women didn't have the mettle to be aviators. "You stuck up for her, didn't you? I thought she was a good friend of yours. Weren't you the one that told her about the job opening here?"

"Well, yeah, I did tell her, but she wasn't all that good

a friend. She was just the daughter of a friend of my mom's, that why I told her about the job with LifeLine. No big deal.''

"So you didn't stick up for her.'' She snorted. She wished she'd been in the restaurant when the others were bad-mouthing Erica, she would have given them something to think about. Jerks. "Well, I don't think Erica had anything to do with the King Air going down. I flew with her for her checkout, and she did just fine.''

"Well, you were at the crash site, what do you think happened?'' Cameron leaned against his locker, arms crossed over his chest.

"I'm not sure what I saw. All I know is that it wasn't her fault.'' She had several ideas about why the copilot hadn't been the cause of the wreck, but she wasn't going to tell him. Not until she was sure.

He shrugged. "It's just like you women to stick together like that. You realize, though, that she really could have been at fault, you just won't say it.''

"Hey, I don't want to get into an argument about it. I'm too tired for that.'' She surveyed the room, eager to find something else to talk about so that the conversation wouldn't end on a sour note. She didn't want to be labeled a bitch by anyone, even if her crankiness was justified.

As her gaze swung past Cameron's locker, her eyes lit on an eight-by-ten photo taped to its steel door, the picture showing a red-and-mustard-gold Piper Super Cub sitting on a gravel-pocked beach. She smiled and leaned forward.

"You're the only guy I know who hangs a picture of a plane on his locker door,'' she said, grinning. "Most guys have tool company calendars that show half-nude women holding up crescent wrenches. That your plane?''

He beamed like a proud papa. "You betcha!'' he crowed. "Nineteen-fifty-seven Super Cub with a beefed-up one-eighty engine! I bought it as a wreck; me and my brother rebuilt and refinished it. You can eat your lunch off the engine block, it's so clean.'' He brushed the picture as though to remove a few grains of invisible dust from it.

Taylor admired the picture, then took a closer look at it when something struck her as odd. Hanging out the aircraft's side window were human legs—rubber swim fins hung off both limbs, looking like webbed feet. "Where the hell did you get a photo like that, anyway?" she asked, laughing. "Is that you there, imitating Kermit the Frog?"

"Yeah, that's me. We flew down to Whittier to do some diving in the Sound. I fell asleep in the airplane after the dive and got those fins stuck on my feet for that goofy photo." He rolled his eyes and slammed the door, appearing to be embarrassed to have her see him looking kind of stupid.

"Who took the photo, a girlfriend or something? They probably had to work at getting you to look like a dork."

"Naw, not a girlfriend. Just my snot-nosed little brother, you met him the other night—"

A heavy grinding noise filled the room, and her eyes darted toward the door to the hangar. "That must be the Lear, back from Seattle." She jumped up to her feet. Steve Derossett was on board the Learjet, and she was dying to talk to him. "I guess I'll go see what's up."

Cameron raised his eyebrows, a smirk on his face, and picked up his flight case. "Later, then. I gotta catch my flight to Seattle. Alaska Airlines still hasn't made it a practice to wait for me." He transferred his flight case to the other hand and turned to exit the room.

Taylor had caught the knowing expression on his face, but she just shrugged it off. Even though she and Steve didn't act like a couple at work—company policy frowned on fraternizing between the employees—she figured everyone knew they saw each other away from the airport. "See you later, Cam," she called to his vanishing back.

SIX

Hurriedly, Taylor pushed the door to the hangar open and stepped through it. A small tug was pulling LifeLine's silver-and-burgundy Learjet into its parking slot, and a similarly painted King Air sat in one of the corners opposite her. Next to the adjoining wall stood several tall cabinets, which held boxes of the common medical supplies that required periodic replenishment on the medevac aircraft. The white surface of the room's concrete floor gleamed, an obvious sign of frequent mopping.

When she caught a glimpse of the aircraft across the room, the twin of the one lying on the side of Mt. Iliamna, her face contorted. She wanted to forget what had occurred, at least for a few moments, but everywhere she turned she saw reminders. Nate had attempted to rid himself of an obvious one, by erasing the names of Erica and Marshall from the scheduling board, but how do you make an airplane vanish?

She walked toward the Learjet, brightening slightly when she saw two men trotting down its airstair. Both Steve Derossett and Kai Huskisson had their navy-blue Nomex flight suits on, which made them look a lot like Maytag repairmen rather than pilots. Had she been in a better mood, she would have smiled when that image crept, uninvited, into her head.

Kai Huskisson was a fairly new addition to the company's flight line, as a Learjet copilot. When he had first reported for duty, she had applauded Nate's decision to employ him—the handsome man easily could have posed as a *Playgirl* centerfold. Even though she had no intention of stepping out on Steve, Kai was certainly entertaining to watch. Early thirties—a few years younger than *her* beau— six feet tall, athletic build, dark curly hair, and a thick walrus mustache. She'd never seen him in anything but his uniform or street clothes, but the way he moved under them filled some of the blanks in her imagination.

The vision of Steve (whom she *had* seen minus uniform or street clothes) and Kai walking in her direction normally would have cheered her immensely, but that wasn't the case that evening.

"Hey, Steve, Kai," she said vacantly when they reached her. "You guys have fun in Seattle?"

The copilot shook his head. "Naw, it was a drag. We can never go anywhere when we're with the Lear, so we have to stay at the airport or the hotel. Steve and I wanted to go out to the track and bet on the horses, but noooo . . ."

"Somebody left a racing form in our room at the hotel," the other man explained, "and we thought we could make some money on the side while we were waiting. We're barely squeaking by on what we get paid, you know how hard it is." He grinned.

She only lifted an eyebrow. The Learjet pilots were paid handsomely—they made a lot more than she did—and she realized the joke was aimed at her. However, she didn't feel like laughing.

Appearing to notice her somber mood, Steve studied her face as the three of them walked across the hangar. The groaning of the big door closing filled the air, covering the muted thud of their footsteps. "Hey, Kai," he commented once the door snapped shut, "go ahead and start your paperwork. I'll be in to sign it in a second."

"Why don't you sign it now, I've got it done. I finished it while we were waiting to cross six-left after our landing. I swear, that JAL freighter took forever getting out of the way, I coulda starved."

Kai offered the clipboard to his captain, and Steve glanced at it briefly before he signed it. "Okay, here you go"—he handed it back—"I'll see you later."

"Sounds good to me. I'm gonna get out of this monkey suit." Kai saluted the older man in mock deference and marched off for the locker room.

As his copilot disappeared, Steve turned to Taylor. "Something wrong?" he asked, peering down at her. At six foot three, he towered over her five foot six. That was one of the things she liked about him, though she was hesitant to admit such traditional male-female attractions affected her. Must be biology, she thought, females being drawn to the robust, tall males, the ones that can bring home a grocery cart full of mammoth steaks.

"I guess you haven't heard about two-three-two going down," she muttered, looking up at him. "It happened last night, crashed on the side of Mt. Iliamna. No survivors." She looked away, not wanting to meet his gaze until she had herself under control. After a few seconds, she inhaled sharply and continued. "Erica and Marshall were up front, Gwen Littleton and Jocelyn Evans in back with the medevac patient. I don't know who the patient was, some Yup'ik guy from Iliamna village. The plane was in pieces."

"Oh, no. Taylor . . ." He pulled her closer to him and buried her in his grasp. "I didn't hear about that, nobody called Seattle to tell us. I can't believe it."

As his firm grip held her, she wished she'd had him with her that morning. "What happened?" he said quietly. "You up to telling me about it?"

She sighed. "*I* sure don't know what happened, Steve. It could be anything—pilot error, a mechanical malfunction. I went down with the troopers and a couple of guys from the Alpine Rescue team this morning to retrieve the bodies, and I poked around a bit while I was there. I didn't see anything obvious that could mean a malfunction, but I'm not a mechanic, so . . . Anyway, as far as pilot error, your guess is as good as mine. We'll have to wait for the NTSB report. I don't think they've gotten down there yet to look at the crash site, so we may not know the cause for some time.''

Withdrawing from his arms, she led him toward the locker room. She felt creepy, surrounded by so much open space, dwarfed by the enormous concrete-walled room, her words bouncing back to her as echoes. She wanted to be somewhere else, somewhere smaller, more confined. More protected.

''You said the crew was Marshall Price and Erica Wolverton?'' When she nodded, he matched her stride and draped an arm over her shoulders. ''I know Marshall pretty well, but not Erica. She was the new hire, wasn't she?''

Averting her eyes, she croaked, ''It was her first flight.''

''Hmmm, a greenhorn.'' He appeared to digest that thought. ''You checked her out, what did you think of her? Did you see her do anything wrong during the checkout, anything that could mean trouble in the future?''

''Hey, I signed her off, didn't I? You think I'm stupid enough to do that if I wasn't sure she had what it took?'' Taylor glared at Steve. She couldn't believe he was toying with the idea that the young woman had contributed to the wreck. She thought she knew him better than that. ''She didn't have anything to do with the King Air going down, trust me. You sound just like the other guys, trying to blame her just because she was a new hire that happened to be a woman.''

They entered the locker room. Kai was nowhere to be seen; she concluded he'd left after changing out of his Roto-Rooter uniform. She planted herself on the empty bench, still scowling.

"Okay, don't go alpha-sierra on me, I wasn't accusing her of anything. I just thought that since she was new to the airplane—"

"Well, you thought wrong," she snapped. She was a bit peeved at him, and that disturbed her. She had been so eager to see him, to discuss her earlier discoveries with him. What the hell happened? Now she sounded like a shrew. Her contentious spirit perplexed her—she didn't think the crash would get to her like *that*.

She attempted to temper her mood, get back to the topic she really wanted to discuss with him. Fingering the bloody tear in her jeans, she composed herself. The calming, deep breath she forced out of her mouth ruffled her bangs.

"How the hell did you do that?" he exclaimed, pointing at her knee. He joined her on the bench and leaned over to examine the scabbed-over gash under the abraded denim.

She pushed his hand away when he tried to prod the wound. "Hey, I'm okay. At least when you don't poke at me. I just got that scrape climbing around in the lava rocks on Iliamna—"

"Lava rock?" He stared her, not sure what she was talking about. Then he relaxed, nodding his head. "Oh, yeah, I'd forgotten that Iliamna was a dormant volcano. . . ."

Cocking her head, she raised an eyebrow. "Well, anyway, the troopers' helicopter couldn't land right next to the wreckage; we had to hike over a pretty steep ridge to get to it. It was a bear getting the bodies back to the helicopter."

Taylor was surprised that she could talk about the scene on the Alaska Peninsula without losing her cool. Maybe her senses were finally becoming dulled. Peering up at Steve, a question arose in her eyes. "I did see some things at the crash site that didn't fit into the usual scenario, you know? It was kinda weird."

"Well, I'm sure the NTSB will figure it out when they go down there to investigate the accident. It'll take forever, but eventually we'll know what happened. I wouldn't worry about it.''

"Yeah, I know I shouldn't worry, but still . . ." The muffled roar of an airliner lifting off from runway six-left rattled the windows in the front office, and they glanced over their shoulders toward the sound. "Anyway," she continued, "have you ever heard of a body turning bright red after dying in a crash? Both Erica and Marshall looked like a couple of radishes when we hauled them out of the cockpit.''

"Yeah, I know what you mean, I've seen it before. I was told that that's just postmortem lividity.'' Steve cracked a smile. "I sound like Dr. Kildare, spouting out medical terminology. I wonder where I got that word from. I can't explain it, but I know what it looks like. I bet one of the flight nurses told me what it was.''

She nodded. "One of the troopers told me about it," she said, then delved into Ferdin's explanation and her disagreement with it. "And even after what I said, nobody could tell me why the pilots were the only ones that were red. I wonder about that. . . .''

Steve shrugged. "I'm surprised there were any bodies to look at in the first place. Unless the plane pancaked onto the slope, a nose-first impact would've destroyed the ship. I've seen pictures of wrecks like that—there's nothing to look at but a pile of tiny fragments.''

"I wondered about that, too. What could've occurred to cause the King Air to hit flat like that? A stall is the only thing I can think of, but why on earth would something like that happen at altitude? Could they have been looking at something on the mountain, lost track of their airspeed? You know, like the moose hunters do during the fall?''

"Well, they wouldn't be looking down, not unless they had their infrared goggles on. You said it happened at night, didn't you? It's starting to get dark sooner now, and I'm sure they couldn't have seen much.''

"Do you suppose some kind of equipment failure was

responsible? I realize that's not likely—I sure didn't see any signs of it—but this was a pretty strange accident." She pondered over the wisdom of telling him of the oddly disfigured airstair door she'd found. As a pilot he'd understand what she was talking about, and as an intimate friend he'd be unlikely to make fun of her if he thought she was blowing the discovery way out of proportion.

"You know, Steve," she said matter-of-factly, trying to make it sound like a second thought, "I found something on the King Air that struck me as unusual. The airstair door had been sheared off the fuselage."

"What's weird about that? You said the airplane was pretty torn up."

"Yeah, but it looked like somebody dissected it. It was . . ." She tried to picture what she'd seen while digging around the battered aircraft. Her gaze narrowed when the image came to her, fuzzy segueing into focused. "The original airstair door had torn away from the larger medevac modification. I would think that if the entire door separated from the fuselage, the two pieces would remain attached. It wasn't that way, though."

"Did the latch get broken off? I know the smaller airstair door can be opened while the larger one is closed by swinging that latch to the side."

"No, the latch was still intact, but I found something else—" She condensed what she had found on the door attachment bolts, hoping he didn't think she was making too much of a big deal out of it.

Cocking his head, he listened to her explanation, then stood. "You're right, that is kinda odd. You said they looked like they'd been cut?" He glanced over his shoulder at her as he began stripping his Nomex flight suit off.

Unfortunately, he had his street clothes on under the flight suit, as he ordinarily did. The coveralls weren't comfortable over bare skin, and she wore hers the same way, over something else.

But the way his jeans molded to him reminded her of

one of the reasons why she missed him when he was gone.

With a stifled sigh, she forced herself to stay on the subject. After all, it was pretty important. "Yeah, those bolts were cut. What do you think about that, anyway? Why would anybody try to tamper with an airstair door? Were they confused about the amount of damage a trick like that could do to the King Air? Like, none? One part of the hatch separating from the other didn't cause the crash."

"Of course it didn't, but hacksaw marks don't appear out of the blue." He crossed one arm across his chest and cradled his chin with the other.

Taylor smiled at his imitation of *The Thinker,* then broke into his pondering. "What do you suppose someone was trying to do?" she asked. "I have no idea, myself. If they were trying to initiate a crash, they sure were confused about how to do it."

Even *she* could have done a better job of sabotaging a King Air than that. "I must be making too much of what I saw; it's probably just something you can explain with a physics text. I'll let the NTSB take a stab at it, that's what they're for. Anyway . . ." She stood up abruptly and pinned him between her body and the wall. Her outstretched arms, planted on the lockers bordering his, kept him from moving. It was fun imitating an aggressive, me-Tarzan-you-Jane male stance—it made her smile and elevated her mood. She really could use the lift.

He glanced at her outstretched arms with an amused expression. "You're not tough enough to get away with that," he murmured, breaking her hold on him. In an opposing gesture, he gripped her wrists behind her back, and leaned down to kiss her.

SEVEN

Pale gray light bled through the window in Taylor's sleeping loft, prompting her to unveil one eye, then the other. The slanted side wall of the A-frame cabin stared back at her from a distance of only several inches—she found herself crammed up against the side of the bed, in a space no wider than her torso. Glancing over her shoulder, she saw Steve sprawled across the mattress, taking up most of the room. His chest rose and fell as he breathed deeply— he was firmly ensconced in dreamland.

"Hey, you're hogging the bed," she complained loudly, with a jab to his side.

"Mmpph," he replied and turned over, freeing a few more square feet of mattress.

"Don't hurt yourself trying to give me some room," she said under her breath. Even though she sounded miffed, she didn't really mind having him steal the covers when he spent the night at her house. She did the same thing to him.

Waking up with another human body nearby—one that always seemed to know what she needed—felt wonderful. She had spent most of the night emptying her brain of the images of the day, and Steve was a good receptacle for that, listening patiently as she talked and talked.

The sex afterwards had been good, too. He'd sensed that she wanted to really let go, to lose herself in something other than thoughts of shattered airplanes and shattered bodies. Their lovemaking had been energetic and passionate—even a bit rough—and she'd welcomed that, for some reason.

Languidly, she studied his well-sculpted back, the result of petitioning him to join her health club and start a weight-training regime. The definition of his muscles was pronounced, but they were sleek and streamlined like a swimmer's, not bulky like a powerlifter's. Just the kind of body she relished touching.

The feel of her hand softly caressing the small of his back was the last sensation she acknowledged before nodding off again.

The piercing *wheep-wheep . . . wheep-wheep . . . wheep-wheep* of Steve's pager rang across the loft. He groaned and sat up in bed, the down comforter tumbling from his chest to puddle in his lap. As it slipped off her shoulders, Taylor rolled over and dragged it back onto her side of the bed. *She* wasn't going to get cold, it wasn't *her* pager that had gone off.

With one hand he brushed his thick blond hair back, and with the other he picked up the pager. After checking the number it displayed, he reached to dial the phone.

She recognized the digits he pressed: the hospital switchboard. "Give me LifeLine operations," she heard him say. Only a few seconds passed before someone came to the transferred call, ready to talk to him.

"This is Steve, I got the page. What's up for me?" he asked. "Uh-huh . . . Uh-huh . . . Okay, I'll call for the Dutch Harbor weather, then take off for the airport. You called Kai Huskisson, right? . . . Okay, he'll probably be waiting for me at the hangar. Later, Shawna." He cradled the phone and stepped out of bed.

"Dutch Harbor, huh? What's happening there?" she questioned, watching him snag his clothes from the floor where he'd tossed them hurriedly last evening. Dutch Harbor, on one of the Aleutian Islands, was a long way off, and she envied him for getting a trip like that. The fishing community of Dutch Harbor nestled in the midst of the chain of volcanic mountains that made up the Aleutians, and the scenery was spectacular. Those volcanoes were not dormant, like Iliamna, but erupted at fairly regular intervals. She hadn't seen one go up, but what a sight *that* would be.

"Yeah, I'm heading for Dutch. Prenatal call." He bent over to lace his boots. "You want to get me some weather?"

"Aye-aye, Captain." She climbed over the castaway comforter and nabbed the phone. The number for Flight Service was etched in her brain, and it came directly to her fingers without a conscious command.

She snatched up a small notebook to copy down the weather while she counted rings and waited to let-her-fingers-do-the-walking. The meteorological forecast system had become automated recently—you fed it numbers using the phone's keypad, which told the computer where you were heading, and it coughed up the current conditions and prediction for the area.

She hated the new system, being used to talking to a real person when she called Flight Service. She had liked that, but now, more often than not, you never talked to anybody during the entire time you were on the phone. As she held the receiver to her ear and listened to a well-modulated recorded voice, she cursed the machinations of the FAA.

During a pause in the weather briefing, she glanced out the window. The light slipping through the pane was brighter than earlier, but no less gray. August was turning out to be rainy, as it nearly always did—old-timers called Alaska's fall the *monsoon season,* and the falls *she* had experienced bore that up.

By the time Steve had his flight jacket on, she had finished scribbling down the weather and handed the slip to him. "Looks a little nicer down there to the southwest," she commented. "You might have a nice flight. You gonna be back later this afternoon?"

He bent down to give her a quick kiss. "I would think so, unless something falls off the Learjet." When he saw her pained expression, he amended his comment. "Sorry, bad joke." He ruffled her hair playfully in his not-too-serious way of interacting with her. She liked gestures like that—it made it a lot easier to subdue her feelings for him when they were at the office.

Zipping his jacket, he added, "I hope you have a better day today than you had yesterday. I'll see you later."

Halfway down the ladder from the loft to the living room, he stopped and peeked over the railing. "You have any plans for today?"

"Yeah, I got some data-input to do. That'll keep me busy for a while. Have a good flight." She watched him duck below the ledge, and heard him cross the floor to the front door. A slam signaled his departure.

With a *plop!* she fell back into bed. She really ought to head for the office, but she wanted a few more minutes of sleep. She'd had it rough the previous day, she deserved it.

By mid-morning, Taylor was staring at a monitor screen, a stack of flight logs piled to her left. The computer and its accessories were arrayed upon an army-surplus table in front of an olive-drab metal chair.

A half-eaten almond bear claw pastry lay on the tabletop, and she grabbed it to jam it into her mouth. As far as she was concerned, there was no ladylike way to eat a bear claw—they were too gooey and tasted too good to worry about consuming them civilly.

She didn't care for the grunt work she was doing, the monthly entry of flight time numbers into the computer's database, but she figured it was worth it. If *that* chore was

the only downside of a job like the one with LifeLine, she'd
do it any day of the week.

Nate sat in his high-back chair, thumbing through the
August issue of *Business and Commercial Aviation.* Only
several hours after being left in a semblance of order, his
desk was well on its way to its usual disarray.

Taylor had glanced at it when she came in earlier, and
arched her eyebrows. What does he do, she thought, purposefully throw papers around first thing in the morning
when he sits down?

The sound of the front door opening prompted her to
swing around to see who had come in. The parking lot
behind the closing door glistened in the gray daylight—the
light rain that had preceded her arrival to the office still
fell. The outside air that blew into the room as the door
swung shut was damp and scented with the smell of wet
asphalt.

A man wearing an expensive three-piece suit, sans rain-
coat or umbrella, stepped up to Nate's desk. The drizzle
had freckled his glasses, making the light bounce off them
like they were part of a kaleidoscope. A beaked nose was
suspended above an incongrously chinless jaw. His faded
blond hair, slicked back over a bald pate, appeared to be
drenched, but Taylor sensed its oily finish came from Bryl-
creem, not raindrops.

His costly suit, and the gold nugget-encrusted watchband
around his wrist, seemed to be a way of compensating for
his physical appearance. He probably drove a Cadillac, too,
she figured. Amazing how men attempt to detract from their
shortcomings like that.

Then she chastised herself—that was unlike her, making
fun of his looks. He couldn't help them. He was probably
just a salesman, stopping by to sell the King Accelerated
Ground School course on videotape.

The man held out a hand for Nate Mueller to shake.
"Michael Westover, National Transportation Safety Board
investigator. You are Mr. . . ."—he glanced at the name-

plate on the desk—"Mr. Mueller? I have some questions concerning the King Air that went down yesterday."

National Transportation Safety Board? She made a one-hundred-and-eighty-degree turnaround in her estimate of Westover. So much for traveling videotape salesman.

She hadn't expected a second call from the NTSB; they'd stopped by the previous day to pick up the maintenance records for the downed King Air. Why would they have more questions about the wreck now? She shifted in her seat. Could it be that the oddities she'd seen the previous day on Mt. Iliamna were important, after all?

Westover aimed a pen at the notepad he held. "I need to speak to the person that trained Miss Wolverton, the one that signed her off to fly the King Air. Who would that be?"

The office manager looked surprised by the question. "That would be Taylor Morgan, our check airman for the King Air."

"Ahhh." Westover jotted something down on his pad, then looked up. "How could I contact him, could you give me his phone number?"

Cracking a grin, Nate shook his head. "No, you don't need to call, that's him sitting over there. He's a she." He pointed at Taylor, who leveled a stare at Westover.

The weaselly-looking man's assumption that a check airman could only be a male didn't impress her. For that reason, because of the confusion that arose when a check air*man* was a woman, she preferred the non-gender-specific title of check pilot.

But at least he didn't call Erica *Mr.* Wolverton, assuming the final *a* in her first name was a typo.

Without even having the diplomacy to blush when he realized his mistake, Westover appraised her. She didn't care for the clinical way he inspected her, like it was his job to examine everything for defects.

She wished she'd dressed more professionally that morning. Even though she didn't have yesterday's torn jeans on, neither was she in a sweater and slacks. Of course, she never had to dress like that at any time, but it would have been nice to feel better about her appearance that morning.

"You had a female check airman training a female copilot, huh?" Westover commented. "How . . . progressive . . . of you."

Flinching, Nate opened his mouth to say something, then closed it. She figured he'd decided it wasn't wise to antagonize the NTSB; they could make it hard on LifeLine if they decided the crash was somehow the company's fault.

"If you would like to interview Miss Morgan without any interruptions, feel free to use that room over there." He pointed to his left, and she noticed the subtle insult of offering the other man the locker room rather than his own desk.

"Okay." Walking over to the other door, Westover gestured at her to follow him. "Miss Morgan . . . ?"

Rolling her eyes for her friend's benefit, she dislodged herself from her seat and joined the bespectacled man in the next room.

As he leafed through his notebook, she planted herself on the end of the wooden bench and attempted to make herself comfortable. She noticed a collection of dust balls in the corner and resolved to attack the linoleum with a mop later. Obviously, whoever was so good about scrubbing the hangar's concrete floor didn't feel responsible for cleaning the office. A job as traditionally female as janitor work didn't appeal to her, but nobody had asked her to do it, so that made it okay.

"So, Miss Morgan—" began Westover.

"Call me Taylor. Miss Morgan sounds like I'm sitting in the principal's office," she confessed. Talking to the man from the NTSB made her uncomfortable, though she didn't know why. She hadn't done anything wrong, so what was it? Maybe she was just sensing his misogynist tendencies.

"So . . . *Taylor* . . . tell me how Miss Wolverton's checkout in the King Air went. Did she feel uncomfortable in a complex aircraft like that?''

''Of course she didn't feel uncomfortable, she didn't have any difficulty with it at any time. After all, she flew the Beech 1900s for Central Alaska Express. Everything I saw her do was professional quality.'' She reported on the entire flight for him as he nodded and took notes. When she got to the landing gear emergency, his eyebrows rose and his pen froze.

''You say she handled that well?'' Westover's mien indicated doubt, and he made his question more specific. ''She didn't have any problems getting distracted and losing track of the airplane during the emergency?''

She hoped her dumbstruck expression would suffice to show him how ridiculous that sounded, but he acted as though he waited for more. ''Erica was just fine,'' she assured him. ''She knew all of her procedures, didn't lose her cool. What else can I say? Why are you asking, anyway?''

The NTSB investigator tapped a finger on his notebook and paused for a moment. Eventually, he spoke. ''Well, did you know she was involved in an incident in Fairbanks? Our records indicate that.'' When Taylor nodded yes, he continued. ''Then you know that she was instructing a student pilot, and that the Cessna trainer they were using taxied into a parked aircraft, substantially damaging it.''

''Big deal. That wasn't her fault. Her student panicked and lost control of the plane, firewalled the throttle and plowed right into a Piper twin. There's no way she could've prevented that.''

Erica had confessed to that incident the first day of training, but Taylor realized that taxiing into a parked plane was fairly innocuous, and shrugged it off.

A shaken head demonstrated Westover's disagreement. ''But as the instructor she was also the pilot-in-command. The PIC always carries the blame for what happens to an aircraft. She should've seen it coming and averted the incident. She panicked, too." He averted his gaze, as though mourning the loss of professionalism shown by the other woman.

Taylor shrugged. "Okay, so something bad happened in her past. We all make mistakes. What the hell does that have to do with the King Air wreck?"

"Well, that shows a pattern of distractibility, a lack of quick reflexes when faced with a troublesome situation."

"I never saw that when I flew with her. She handled the gear problem no sweat. What could have panicked her in the King Air, anyway? As far as we know, they were flying straight and level before they hit."

The NTSB investigator consulted his notes, perhaps to buy himself some time before answering her question. "Okay. Do you remember seeing Marshall Price wearing an oxygen mask? Trooper Hall told me about it." She nodded, and he resumed. "We believe that Price suffered a heart attack—"

"A heart attack?" Befuddled by that information, her expression shifted into confusion. "He just passed a first-class flight physical. How could he have done that if he was on the verge of having a heart attack?" She remembered what Marshall had looked like the last time she'd seen him—not a smidgen of fat on his body. For a forty-something divorced male, not only was that impressive, it was not likely to point toward organ failure.

"Have you ever heard of IHSS? Idiopathic hypertrophic sub-aortic stenosis? The pathologist that performed the autopsy on Price found signs of IHSS, and believes he had a heart attack sometime during the flight. Hence, Gwen Littleton being found near Price's body—she was administering oxygen while helping him."

"But why didn't he show some symptoms? He wasn't overweight, he didn't smoke, he watched his diet—"

"That's what idiopathic means: of unknown cause. It can kill you without any warning. Not until an autopsy is performed, and an enlarged heart is discovered, can IHSS be detected. Price may not have been dead before the aircraft hit the mountain, but he was certainly incapacitated.''

Taylor gaped at Westover—she'd never heard of a hidden killer like that. Without thinking, she placed her hand on the left side of her chest—could that IHSS thing happen to her?—then caught herself and withdrew it. That was a pretty lame move, she conceded.

"But even if Marshall had a heart attack,'' she prompted, "why'd the plane go down without Erica alerting Center to an emergency? Anyway, she could've handled the plane by herself, I wouldn't have signed her off if I hadn't been sure of that.''

"Well, you might've been wrong. She could have panicked and gotten distracted—lost track of her airspeed, altitude, and course—and before she knew it she was staring at the side of Mt. Iliamna from very close range. The rest is history.''

Shaking her head, she disagreed—there were holes in the story. "Okay, say your theory is true, Erica wasn't paying attention to the airplane. Hell, she was probably damn worried about Marshall, and that was getting to her, but why didn't Center call her when they saw her change course and altitude without contacting them? It was an IFR flight, after all, they were under radar control—''

"Hey, we checked the radios when we went to the crash site, looking specifically for why that didn't happen. The copilot's radio was tuned to a frequency other than Center, the captain's radio was the one tuned to ARTCC. Apparently, Erica forgot to change the tuning of her radio when she took over the command of the plane. ARTCC called the King Air, several times, but were unable to raise them. They watched the airplane go off course, then disappear from the radar screen.''

Taylor shuddered, imagining the final moments for the plane, when the young copilot realized what had happened. What had she been thinking?

EIGHT

Taylor sat, paralyzed, on the locker room bench. She suddenly realized that her head pounded—a strong *thump!thump!thump!* accompanied her heartbeat. Glancing up at the lockers, she strained to read the name tags on them through eyes blurred by tears that refused to break free. She felt as though it was very important for her to focus on those insignia, to prevent the tears from spilling out of her eyes. Westover hadn't shown her that he was someone likely to tolerate the display of tears—undoubtedly, he'd scoff at *female fragility*. Hearing of airplane wrecks, even those with multiple fatalities, probably didn't faze him at all.

The NTSB investigator closed his notebook and stood. "Well, I guess that'll be my preliminary finding: pilot error. Miss Wolverton lost track of the aircraft's location when distracted by her captain's heart attack. I'm sorry that happened, but . . ." He marched out of the locker room, stopping to tell Nate Mueller of his conclusion, and to ask for the keys to Erica's Geo. He wanted to check the vehicle for signs of drug or alcohol abuse that could relate to the copilot's distractibility.

The front door squeaked open as he stepped into the parking lot, and thudded closed, stifling the jangle of keys in his hand.

In a matter of seconds, Nate had bounded from his chair and dropped next to Taylor on the locker room's bench. "Wasn't that guy a slime?" he pronounced, wrapping one arm around her shoulders. "Saying it was Erica's fault. Shit. Now he's looking for drugs."

Shrugging out from underneath her friend's arm, she shook her head. "Oh, don't say that to me, just to make me feel better. It sounds like he's got the facts on his side. I musta screwed up, not seeing any problem with Erica's flying." She rested her hands on her thighs, elbows akimbo, and stared at the lockers. When she glanced at the name tag that still read Erica Wolverton, she pushed off the bench and stood. "I gotta get out of here. I'll finish up with those flight times tomorrow. Just leave the pile on the table where they are, okay?"

After studying her face, he nodded. She snatched her flight jacket from the coatrack in the other room and stalked out the door.

When she glanced across the parking lot, she saw Westover standing next to the dead woman's compact car, talking to an aged man and woman. He concluded the conversation, handed the Geo's keys to the gray-haired man, and turned away. The woman, probably the older man's wife, reached out and grabbed the keys, and lifted them to her face as if they were a religious artifact. Even from some distance, Taylor could see the red circling the woman's eyes.

Immediately, she knew they were Erica's parents.

She dashed across the lot toward the couple, unsure of what to say, but *very* sure that she wanted to say something. The pair were heading for the LifeLine office, and she met them halfway.

"You must be Erica's parents," she stammered when she stopped in front of them. "I'm Taylor Morgan. I didn't

know Erica very well—I only met her a few days ago—
but I liked her a lot and I'm very saddened by her death.
I wanted to deliver my condolences to you.''

"Thank you, from both of us." The elder man bobbed
his head somberly and nodded at his wife. "I'm Eric Lindstrom, and this is Edna." He unconsciously kneaded a nar-
row-brimmed hat as he studied his spouse. She was crying
quietly.

Like his wife, the eyes of Erica's dad were reddened,
and his clothes and hair were rumpled. In addition, Edna
had dark circles under her eyes that spoke of sleepless
nights.

Mr. Lindstrom dragged his head away from the sight of
his weeping wife and aimed his world-weary eyes at Taylor. "Erica mentioned you," he intoned, "when she called
to tell us about her new job. She said you were nice, that
you were real fair. She admired you.''

Taylor blushed, a bit embarrassed. She didn't feel she
deserved to hear compliments from the parents of a woman
that had just died. Especially since *she* might have been a
small factor in that death. "Will there be a service for Erica?" she asked. "I'd like to attend."

Erica's mom fished a hanky out of her purse and blew
her nose before answering. "Yes, there will be a memorial
service for her in Fairbanks. When we have it arranged,
we'll call with the time and date." The mention of the
funeral seemed to trigger another bout of tears, and she
nestled into her husband's arms for comfort as tears coursed
down her cheeks.

"My wife is pretty distraught," the grim-faced man explained. "This is going to be hard, collecting Erica's things
from her locker. She couldn't even bring herself to look at
the car a minute ago. I may just leave her out here in our
Eagle.''

Nodding, Taylor murmured sympathetically. She knew
how the silver-haired woman felt—she'd had difficulty
looking at the Geo, too. "Why don't I just go with you to

get her things, okay? I don't want you to have to rummage around any more than you have to. You can leave your wife here, where she'll feel more comfortable.'' She felt terrible for Erica's parents—offering to escort the older man to the locker room was the least she could do.

After helping the teary-eyed woman into the passenger seat of a white Eagle station wagon, she led Erica's bedraggled dad to the office. During the walk, he apologized for Edna's less-than-social behavior. Of course, Taylor understood—it was hard to be well-mannered when you're dealing with mind-numbing grief.

Eric Lindstrom followed Taylor through the office and into the locker room. When he caught sight of the wide tape strip bearing the name Erica Wolverton, he had to pause to gather himself before opening the door. Even so, there wasn't anything disturbing in there, nothing but an empty plastic earplug container and a change of clothes.

With the neatly folded T-shirt and jeans stacked over one arm, Mr. Lindstrom sighed and swung the door closed. His drooped posture seemed so tragic, as though the small pile of clothes he held weighed a ton.

In a way perhaps it did weigh a ton, holding the burden of his dead daughter's memory.

"Is there anything else I can do for you, Mr. Lindstrom?'' Taylor asked. "Anything at all?''

He shook his head, then paused. "Well, yes, there is something you can do. Erica's brother is going to pick the Geo up and take it back to school with him—''

"Is that Michael, the one going to Stanford?''

"Yes. I guess Erica mentioned him.'' Mr. Lindstrom glanced sadly at the strip of tape on the locker, then looked down. "Anyway, Michael can't get away until Christmas break, and I'd appreciate it if you could look after the car, run it once in a while. Drive it whenever you want to.'' He handed her the keys.

She couldn't see herself driving Erica's Geo—she couldn't even look at it right then—but she nodded vigorously and accepted the keys. "Of course, sir, I'll keep an eye on it. No problem."

He nodded, mumbled good-bye, and trudged back to the parking lot and his waiting wife.

A minute later, after tossing the Geo's keys to Nate with a shake of her head, she was ready to begin her journey home. Walking to her car, she felt like shit—the last several hours had felt like a week. She needed some time alone.

Her Suzuki sat on the far side of the parking lot, as she hadn't wanted to park next to the Geo again like she'd done the previous day. As painful a reminder as it had been earlier, now that she knew what had happened to the King Air, it became a more dreadful one. She hiked across the lot, her gaze fixed on anything but the small vehicle.

After she clambered into her car and keyed the ignition, she huddled in the seat for a moment with her wet bangs dripping water down her forehead. The light drizzle had metamorphosed into a steady downpour, a rarity for South-central Alaska, and she never thought to put a hat on. Even though it rained frequently in Anchorage in August, the rain usually came in the form of sprinkles.

However, the sky had turned against convention. The dark clouds overhead hung low and ominous, and when they opened, the *ping* of raindrops hitting the thin convertible roof of the Suzuki soothed Taylor's rattled brain. With a shove, she engaged the shift lever and directed the car from the lot.

With no destination in mind but *somewhere else,* she put her mind on autopilot. Force of habit led her onto International Airport Road, then onto the six-lane divided Minnesota Drive.

She remembered when Minnesota was nothing but a road that weaved through a muskeg swamp. Anchorage had grown so much, from a town of 75,000, twenty years earlier, to a city of 225,000. Every year the metropolitan sprawl engulfed another swatch of forest, but it still only took a half hour to drive to virtual wilderness. And no degree of urbanization could wipe out the spectacular Chugach Range that loomed over the city.

As she sped down Minnesota, she reached the point where it made a wide ninety-degree arc and segued into O'Malley Road. Her ears popping, she turned up the steep thoroughfare and began a steady climb to her cabin. She hadn't consciously intended to do that—her mind was still in neutral—but once again convention dictated to her.

Shrugging—home was as good a destination as anywhere else—she continued.

As she drove up O'Malley toward the Hillside, she let her mind wander and contemplate the environs. It felt good to empty her mind for a few minutes.

Midway up the hilly road, she passed the Alaska Zoo, with its complement of Alaskan animals—bears, foxes, sheep, otters, even a few caribou and moose. The zoo's former stars, a male and a female polar bear, had died recently from *toxoplasmosis,* a deadly viral infection they had mysteriously encountered. When she thought of their grisly, unexpected deaths, a teardrop grew in her eye, and she brushed it away like flicking an annoying hair back.

If she couldn't even permit herself to cry about the deaths on Mt. Iliamna, how could she weep over a pair of bears?

NINE

Five minutes later, Taylor steered off the asphalt onto a path through the trees. Her Suzuki bounced and bumped over the ruts in her dirt driveway, its motor hiccuping when she turned it off and disengaged the clutch. Reaching up from the wheel, she rubbed her temples—her head still throbbed. Not even her relief at being back at her cabin could soothe the ache.

She felt terrible. All along, she hadn't felt any involvement in the previous day's disaster, but Westover had intimated she should. He didn't come out and say that she'd screwed up by signing Erica off, but she could read in between the lines.

Why hadn't she noticed any clues to future trouble in the other woman's handling of the King Air? Surely, there would have been a sign, if the young copilot had been destined to die in a plane crash caused by her own inattention.

Had she been too lax in evaluating Erica's performance? Had she, unconsciously, cut her coworker some slack, just because she wanted her to succeed? She thought she was a good, fair check pilot, able to overlook trifling details if they didn't really matter. But had she overlooked a detail that was much more important?

Gripping the steering wheel, she set her jaw. No, she hadn't overlooked any pertinent details, regardless of what Westover had implied. She believed in herself, she believed in Erica's abilities, and she *didn't* believe what the NTSB investigator professed to be the truth. Pilot error wasn't at the root of the accident, and she was going to figure out why. Too many things were unusual about the fatal wreck—it couldn't have been a simple crash.

The car door squeaked as she pushed it open and jumped to the ground. As she stared at the door and swung it back and forth a few more times, she resolved to grease it soon and poked at it some more. When she felt the raindrops splattering on the shoulders of her flight jacket, she gave up her examination and plodded toward her front door.

Two clumps of wild iris framed the cabin's stoop, their royal purple blooms standing at attention in the drizzle. She remembered Erica commenting on the irises planted in front of the hotel bar they'd visited after her checkout in the King Air.

As Taylor admired her iris in passing, a picture of Erica during that checkout flight flashed across her mind—she could see the young woman hunched over, pumping vigorously on the landing gear extension lever to lower them manually.

Something about that picture was important. What was it?

The likeness of her copilot came into focus, bent over the extension lever, one hand holding her ill-fitting radio headset in place to prevent it from falling off.

Taylor stopped in mid-stride.

Erica had been fumbling with her radio headset the night of the checkout flight, but when Taylor examined her body at the crash site, the copilot hadn't had it on at all. It had been nowhere to be seen. Obviously, she must have purposefully removed it and tucked it into a nearby cranny.

If Erica was in command of the aircraft when it crashed, as Westover suspected, there would be no reason for her to have taken her headset off. Why would she do that?

There was no proper response to that . . . unless she had to place something *else* over her face.

Taylor had encountered the same problem in the past— she always had to take her David Clark radio headset off when she had to fit something underneath it.

With a start, she realized what she had just said—you could never wear the radio headset over other gear. Other gear, like *an oxygen mask.*

Masks were on *both* pilots when the King Air crashed, even though it hadn't appeared so at first glance. Marshall Price had been wearing his mask for the same reason his copilot did, not because he was having a heart attack.

But why would they have their masks on? And where had Erica's gone?

Taylor stooped to sit down on the cabin's rain-speckled front porch. Her mind whirled, one thought bouncing off another, then something clicked. She recalled the hack-sawed airstair door attachment bolts, which hadn't meant anything at the time. But now, knowing about the oxygen masks, it made perfect sense.

The King Air was a pressurized aircraft, and that meant the differential between the cabin and outside air pressures was substantial at higher altitudes. Substantial enough to break metal parts, if they were substandard in strength to begin with.

Like the partially severed bolts.

At some time during the flight, the weak bolts had allowed the airstair seal to rupture, and the pressure inside the aircraft had been lost. Just as in a commercial airliner, things started happening when that occurred.

In her head, Taylor could hear the well-modulated voice of a flight attendant cooing, ''In the case of a drop in cabin air pressure, a mask will drop down from a compartment above your head. Pull down on it to start the flow of oxygen, then place the mask over your nose and mouth and breathe normally. . . ."

That's why Marshall and Erica had their masks on. The King Air wreck was more than a simple accident caused by pilot error, somebody *wanted* it to crash.

Leaping up from the porch, Taylor yelled, "That's it!" Her shriek startled the raven perched on a nearby birch tree, and it flapped off to a calmer area.

She fumbled in her jeans pocket for her key, muttering impatiently, "Where is it, where is it?" She had to get to the phone, call the NTSB, tell that slimy Westover that he wasn't going to wreck Erica's reputation by blaming her for the crash, there was more to it! Not only would she clear the other woman's name, it would clear *her* name, too.

Once the front door slammed shut behind her, she tore her jacket off and dashed toward her cordless phone. Balancing the receiver between her shoulder and her chin, she thumbed through the phone book for the NTSB's number. Damn, she cursed, why hadn't Westover given her his card? She didn't have time to search for anything.

Finally, she located the number and started to dial. But halfway through the digits, she hesitated and stopped. Wait a second, she thought . . .

She glanced at the phone in her hand and set it back in its stand without completing the call. The same question remained: Why did the King Air slam into the side of Mt. Iliamna? The loss of cabin pressure couldn't have caused the crash. That was a piece of useful information, but not the solution to the $64,000 question.

As she mentally picked at the intertwined pieces of the enigma, she wandered into the kitchen. She loved that room, even though she wasn't much of a gourmet cook, because it was a bright part of the house. White cabinets with light oak trim, white counters supporting brightly colored appliances, bright ash wood flooring. The alabaster tones gave the small cubicle a large feeling, as though it was twice its actual size. Even a simple meal like spaghetti and garlic bread was fun to make, surrounded by such clean lines.

Distractedly, she cut a slice of sunflower seed bread and popped it into the toaster. As she stood by the counter, knife and jelly jar in her hands, the phone rang. She glanced at the toast, browning away, and walked to the phone.

"Hello?" Carrying the phone back into the kitchen, she waited for her toast to come up.

"Miss Morgan? This is Trooper Hall, getting back to you about the question you had yesterday."

"Question?" Her brain must have turned to mush, she didn't recall a question. "Could you be more specific?"

"Uh, yes, I can. You were concerned about the reddish tinge you saw on the pilots' faces at the crash site, you wanted me to check on what it could be, other than post-mortem lividity."

The haze lifted after a second, and she remembered the question. She rubbed her forehead—it was getting hard to separate all the questions she'd encountered in the past thirty-six hours. "Ah, yes, I recall now. What did you find out?"

Hall cleared his throat. "I spoke to the medical examiner doing the autopsy. He said that the cherry-red color could be brought on by carbon monoxide poisoning."

"Carbon monoxide poisoning?" The toast popped up, distracting her for a moment, but she turned away from it to concentrate on the phone call. "But the King Air is pressurized. How could CO get in?" She'd heard of CO poisoning happening in smaller aircraft, because they weren't pressurized. A cracked exhaust manifold on an unpressurized aircraft could force the deadly, odorless CO gas into the cockpit, resulting in asphyxiation for the pilot and passengers.

But nothing could leak into the King Air from outside.

The trooper appeared to be reading her mind. Maybe he knew airplanes, too. "I have no idea how CO could get into the King Air, Miss Morgan, it *is* a pressurized aircraft. I think the color *was* due to lividity.''

"But can the doctor test for CO, just in case? Stranger things have happened." There were numerous unusual factors involved in the fatal crash, and she didn't want to rule anything out just because logic implied something else.

"The doctor has already done that. He's sent a blood sample off for toxicology testing. They'll look for a number of things in it. Alcohol, drugs . . .''

"Ahh. Then we'll know for sure in a few days.''

"Well, we won't know in a few days, try three weeks. These tests take time.''

"Three weeks?" she sputtered. "What's the point, if it takes that long?''

"Why are you concerned about the amount of time it takes? We're not investigating a crime here. From what I saw at the autopsy, we're talking about an ordinary heart attack that had some unfortunate ramifications. I'm sorry, but . . .''

"Yeah, I'm sorry, too. Thank you for calling me back, though.'' She clicked the phone off and stared at her cold toast. "Aw, shit,'' she muttered, partly about the toast, partly because she wasn't getting any answers about the crash. She'd hoped Hall's phone call would resolve something.

She left the cold toast sitting on the counter and headed back into the living room. She had to unravel the ball that was her examination of the accident. She owed it to Erica to clear her name—the crash had a more sinister origin than the one seized upon by Westover.

Somewhere lay the answer to the riddle, but she was starting to wonder if her brain was up to finding it. She'd had so much junk thrown at her, her head was almost overwhelmed.

Plopping down on one of the love seats in her small living room, she let her dejected mood get the better of her. She was getting tired of thinking about this accident without finding any useful clues—maybe she should just give up.

Then she glared at her reflection in the windowpane. No, she wouldn't quit, there was too much at stake. Erica's reputation, and even her own, didn't mean much to Westover, so he wasn't going to go out of his way to amend his findings about the accident, but *she* could.

The crash hadn't been Erica's fault; too many other factors were involved, too many questions were unresolved.

First, how did carbon monoxide get into a pressurized aircraft, in sufficient quantities to leave its telltale red signature on both captain and copilot?

Second, why was the airstair door tampered with? Obviously, somebody had wanted it to pop off in flight. Why?

Then the answer leaped into her consciousness. Somebody wanted the hatch to break free in order to cause the loss of pressure, and to get the pilots to don their oxygen masks. However, instead of getting pure oxygen from the masks, Marshall and Erica got *one hundred percent carbon monoxide.*

They had initiated a steep descent to a lower altitude, put their masks on, and *wham!* In a matter of seconds, they had asphyxiated. No wonder the King Air smacked into Mt. Iliamna—the pilots were dead, nobody was *flying* it.

And that explained the presence of Gwen Littleton in the cockpit. She realized the pilots were incapacitated when the plane began to veer off course and dropped out of the sky, and she came forward in a feeble attempt to do something. She must have been trying to climb into Erica's seat, and pulled the younger woman's oxygen mask off as she struggled to get her out of the way.

Taylor shivered, imagining the last seconds of the tragic flight. Surely, Gwen's ears were popping rapidly as the suddenly unpressurized aircraft dove to the earth, wind shrieking through the breach between the two doors. The screams of Jocelyn Evans, and maybe the guttural croaks of the

Yup'ik man on the stretcher, must have been filling the cabin.

And Gwen couldn't do anything to stop their plummet groundward.

The unbearable image that passed across Taylor's mind was numbingly clear, and she pressed her hands against her face as she broke out in a cold sweat.

Now that she had the answers she'd been searching for, she wished she could go back in time, just an hour, to when she didn't know the truth about the last seconds of the five lives. "Why didn't I just leave it alone?" she wailed to the empty room.

Then the crux of the matter hit her. Who had done this, single-handedly ended the lives of five innocent humans?

TEN

As Taylor slumped in the love seat, her mind striving to decode the message in the accident facts—like *who?* and *why?*—the *wheep-wheep . . . wheep-wheep . . . wheep-wheep* of her pager ripped into the still air.

"Ack!" she squealed, startled. The adrenaline burst accompanying her shock washed over her body, and her eyes narrowed. "Damn, I hate that!" she complained, then picked up the pager from the end table. The digital readout displayed the phone number for the hospital.

She picked up her phone and dialed. "LifeLine operations, please," she requested of the switchboard operator. Two seconds later, she was talking to Shawna, the dispatcher for emergency services. "This is Taylor, whatcha got for me?"

"Adult male in Homer, heart attack. Any problem with a flight down there?"

"No, I don't think so. The weather's a bit crummy here in town, but still flyable. I'll head for the airport. Who's going with me?"

"Let's see . . ." Taylor could picture Shawna swiveling

to check the status board on the wall. "Bonnie Tompkins and Debby Feldberg."

"Hmmm. I know Bonnie, but Debby must be new."

"Yeah, Debby's new, but she went on medevacs out of Seattle. This isn't her first trip out of Anchorage, either; she's gone on a few flights with the other pilots. She's no greenhorn."

Satisfied, Taylor nodded. She knew she wouldn't be up to introducing a new flight nurse to medevacs that day. For that matter, she wasn't even sure she wanted to *go* on a medevac that day, at all. However, as preoccupied with the crash as she was, it might be good to lose herself in her work for a few hours.

"Okay, Shawna, I'll get the weather, head to the airport. Is Cam back on the schedule yet, or am I flying with someone else today? I know he went to Seattle to get the new King Air."

"Well, Todd's name is on the board for daytime duty; I guess Cam's still gone."

"Hmmm. Well, Todd's an okay guy, too. I better get going." She ended the conversation with the dispatcher, then redialed, ready to listen to the prerecorded weather broadcast.

Twenty minutes later, she jogged into the LifeLine office, waved at Nate Mueller, and headed directly for the hangar. Her drive into the Anchorage Bowl from the Upper Hillside had been a bit faster than usual—she was still wired from her upsetting morning—but it wasn't too hazardous. The showers from earlier had dissipated, letting the streets dry, so she didn't worry about losing control on slick asphalt.

The grayness and low cloud covering remained, though, and she realized the flight to Homer would be done on instruments, without any reference to the terrain below. That was okay—if she had to concentrate on the demanding

IFR navigation she wouldn't be able to dwell on anything else.

After assuring herself that Todd Zemanek was busy readying the King Air for the flight, she ducked back into the locker room to don the navy-blue Nomex coverall all of the medevac pilots wore.

Darting back into the hangar a minute later, she saw Todd completing his preflight inspection of the aircraft. He used to seem so out of place doing that—when hired, he hadn't looked old enough to be part of a flight crew—and the first time she met him, she'd taken him as one of the teenage ramp helpers. But when he grew a healthy mustache, and clipped his brown hair, he looked more like twenty-seven, his real age. Not even his slight build could confuse people now.

"We almost ready, Todd?" she asked upon approaching the aircraft. "Where are the nurses?" She scanned the hangar for a few seconds until she spied two bodies next to the tall metal cabinets holding the medical supplies.

"Hey, Bonnie, Debby! Need any help?" She stooped under the King Air's wing and crossed the hangar, ready to aid the women in their struggle with a portable defibrillator and a handheld oxygen dispenser. Even though both women were athletic in their builds, they had their hands full.

"No, we almost got it," Debby grunted. In her early forties, she was the older of the two nurses, and her prematurely gray hair made her look very authoritative. The Kewpie-doll features of redheaded Bonnie made her appear to be junior to Debby, but in fact they were equals.

As Taylor followed them to the King Air, and opened the wide hatch so they could load the equipment inside the cabin, she heard some shouts from the office side of the hangar. She could make out Nate's voice warning someone, and a second later the door from the locker room burst open.

"Hey, leave her alone!" the office manager was yelling.

"Can't you see she has to get out of here right away? She's on a medevac, for chrissake!" He grappled with a dark-haired man she didn't recognize, but though the two men were nearly equal in height and weight, the bearded stranger had the advantage due to his determination.

When the intruder broke away from Nate, he barreled across the hangar toward Taylor, her coworker close on his heels. "Goddamn you!" the angry man barked. "She was too young to die, she shouldn't even have been on that flight! What did you think you had to prove, signing her off to fly like that?"

His expression and aggressive moves scared her—she stepped behind one of the aircraft's wings to put some distance between them. "Hey, whoa!" she said coolly, trying to appease him. To Nate she asked, "Who is this guy?"

"Hey, I'm sorry, Taylor. I couldn't stop him. This is, uh . . . Erica's, uh, husband."

The dangerous-looking man skidded to a stop on the other side of the wing protecting Taylor. Fortunately, he didn't attempt to grab her, but stood there with his fists clenched, breathing hard. "I talked to the NTSB," he growled. "I know they think Erica caused that crash because she forgot to watch what was going on. If she'd known enough about that King Air that wouldn't have happened. She wouldn't have been distracted, even if somebody *was* having a heart attack." He lifted a fist and pounded on the wing. "She wasn't ready to fly that airplane, you should've seen that, you shouldn't have allowed her to go! It's your fault she's dead!"

Taylor's face blanched. Obviously, the stranger believed Westover, and he, too, thought she'd screwed up in her estimate of Erica's abilities. Even though she knew the copilot hadn't caused the wreck, it still hurt to have others blame her for putting the other woman in that situation in the first place. She held up her hands, trying to placate the red-faced man. "Hey, your wife could handle the King Air, that wasn't a problem. It's not that much different than the

1900s, and she'd been flying those for a long time before we hired her."

The stranger glared at her, a vein in his forehead throbbing. "She shouldn't have been flying the 1900, either, that's too much airplane for a girl! I told her that when she got a job with Central Express. She should've listened to me!"

Taylor's eyebrows rose. No wonder Erica separated from that jerk; *she* would have tried to get away from him, too. Nobody told *her* what to do, especially a husband—marriage was a democracy, not a dictatorship.

As she contemplated saying something about the real reason for the crash, she saw Nate Mueller approaching with the security guard from next door in tow. "Mr. Wolverton," he cautioned, "if you don't get away from Miss Morgan, I'll have you removed. By force, if necessary. She has a job to do, you can't be harassing her. Come with me. . . ." Her coworker reached out and snagged Wolverton's elbow.

"Get away from me," the distraught man bellowed, yanking his elbow away. "I'm not doing anything wrong. She's responsible for my wife's death, and I'm going to let her know what I think!"

Turning to the security guard, a beefy ex-Marine with a crew cut, Nate nodded. "Take him outta here." The heavyset man lunged at Wolverton and wrapped him in a bear hug. With Wolverton screaming, he dragged him toward the door.

"Sorry, Taylor," Nate said, "I didn't know who he was at first, and I didn't realize he was after you." He glanced at the struggling pair and ran to catch up with them.

"Goddamn it, you as good as killed her!" Erica's husband screamed as the guard shoved him through the door. "I hope you can live with that—"

She shook her head, her eyes agape. "Damn, what was that all about?" She turned to look at Todd and the nurses, who were shuffling about, dumbstruck by the spectacle they'd witnessed. "I thought Erica was separated from him."

Cocking her head, Bonnie nodded at the door Wolverton had disappeared through. "Well, Erica may have been separated from him, but maybe he wasn't so sure he was separated from her. I've heard about men like that, the kind that think a wife is a piece of property. They never want to let them go. I bet he was abusing her, too."

"Well, he can't do that anymore." Taylor ducked under the wing and stepped up to the aircraft's fuselage. "Anyway, we gotta get going to Homer. This medevac won't wait."

Two hours later, LifeLine's remaining King Air was sitting on a taxiway that branched off one of the main runways at Anchorage International. "Anchorage ground," Taylor recited. "Lifeguard three-lima-lima is cleared of six-left at golf, taxi to the north ramp."

"Lifeguard three-lima-lima, Anchorage ground, cleared to taxi as requested, traffic is a Northern Air Cargo DC-6 taxiing for takeoff, six-right."

"Traffic in sight. Good evening." She released the push-to-talk button on her control yoke and turned to speak to Todd Zemanek. "Take us home," she sighed.

She felt a bit fatigued, even though the trip to Homer had been uneventful and routine. As she had suspected, the instrument flying required by the low cloud cover had kept her occupied for the entire flight, either performing it herself or keeping track of Todd when he was in charge of the navigation. As captain of the aircraft, she was responsible for everything that happened with it, regardless of whether she was doing the actual hands-on flying or not.

But she *had* gotten a reprieve from worrying about her earlier discovery. Only a few hours, but enough to do her some good. She hoped Steve was back from Dutch Harbor so she could discuss it with him.

When Todd taxied the aircraft onto LifeLine's parking

square, she saw an ambulance standing by, its lights flashing, the paramedics alert. Once the propellers had stopped their rotation, the men were scrambling for the aircraft, ready to whisk the patient to the ambulance.

"Thanks for the ride," Bonnie joked as she jumped down to the asphalt from the aircraft's cabin.

"Yeah," seconded Debby, "nice flight." She hurriedly jogged over to Bonnie, obviously eager for the ambulance trip to the hospital.

As Taylor and Todd collected their maps and approach plates from inside the cockpit, Doug the ramp hand towed their plane into the hangar. While he maneuvered it into its parking space, she glanced out the window and spotted the Learjet perched in a corner. "Good, Steve's back," she murmured to herself. "I got a lot to tell him."

"What?" Todd asked, looking up from his flight case. "You say something?"

"Uh-uh, just talking to myself." She grinned at him cheerfully. "Occupational hazard. You'll see what I mean one of these days."

Totally confused by her remark, her copilot bent over to lock the hasps on his bag. "Okay, whatever you say. I'll leave the flight log in the office for you to sign, then I'm taking off. Hot date tonight." He stood and leered at her.

She envied him, being so caught up in young romance. She couldn't even remember the last time she had anticipated a hot date. Not that her relationship with Steve wasn't great, but she'd matured in the past years and didn't fall into the excited-by-a-date mode anymore. "See ya later, Todd. Have fun tonight. By the way, you got any condoms?"

He gaped at her and stammered, "C-c-c-condoms?" before he realized she was playing with him and broke into a grin. "Of course, Taylor. Gotta whole box of 'em, neon ones. Glow in the dark. . . ." He smirked at her, walked back to the airstair, and trotted down it. With a wave, he saundered across the hangar floor and vanished through the locker room door.

Ahh, young love.

She collected her gear and stuffed it in her flight case, as she thought about calling Steve. Maybe she'd just drive over to his house, surprise him with what she'd put together concerning the King Air accident. Her detective work would impress him.

When she pushed the locker room door open and stepped inside, she peered around the corner into the front office. She expected to see Nate Mueller sitting behind his desk, but instead a pair of lanky legs, propped on the computer table, caught her eye. "Hey, Steve, just the person I was looking for!" she called out to the size-twelve feet.

Throwing her flight case on the bench, she trotted toward the door. "I got something I gotta tell you. About the King Air wreck."

Marching into the front room, she shoved his feet off the table and traded places with them. "We got a visit from the NTSB this morning, one of their investigators, named Westover. He was looking for me, and . . ." She condensed the conversation for Steve, going over the autopsy results on Price, ending with the NTSB investigator's implication that she should have seen the clues to trouble with Erica.

"But that's bullshit," she argued, "because I figured out what really happened."

The tall, blond man leaned forward in his chair, astonishment in his features. "How'd you come to a different conclusion than the NTSB? They're the experts."

"Well, yeah, but Westover has decided what the truth is, and he's closed his mind.

"Anyway, here's what I put together." She sketched her late morning activities for him, concluding with the phone call from Trooper Hall and how the answer to the riddle just hit her once she'd hung up. With a big grin, she stopped talking and began to shed her Nomex coveralls, assuming he had followed her comments. It all seemed so simple to her, like connecting the dots.

"But I thought the autopsy showed Price died from a heart attack. How do you account for that?" he asked, puzzled.

"Hey, the autopsy showed signs of IHSS, but there was no proof that IHSS actually killed him. It was really the CO that killed him, and Erica, too."

"So you think the masks were delivering carbon monoxide to the pilots rather than oxygen?" He shook his head, perplexed. He didn't appear to be reaching the same conclusion to the facts she had poured over. He leaned back in his chair. "But how would anybody be able to exchange CO for oxygen in the system? I've never heard of that being done. You'd have to be a fairly knowledgeable mechanic to figure that out. Are you saying some *worker bee* plotted to bring the King Air down? Why?"

"Well," she muttered, peering at the coverall dangling from her waist, "I haven't gotten that far yet—"

"That seems like an important factor," he said, raising his eyebrows. "The same applies to tampering with the airstair door. There are warning lights that alert the pilots if the door seal is compromised—I *know* that's not news to you—and you'd *have* to be a mechanic to know how to saw through the bolts without tripping one of those circuits. First time the ship is started, those warning lights would go off. There's no way the door could be rigged to fail without bypassing the electrical system. . . ."

She set her jaw and balanced herself on the edge of the table so she could pull one leg out of her flight suit. "Well, I don't know exactly how they did it, but I'm sure that's what was done. Everything fits." The coverall leg snagged on her boot, and she jerked on it to free the foot. "I'll just talk to one of our mechanics, ask *him* how it was done."

"Oh, yeah? One of *our* mechanics? If it would take a mechanic to tamper with the systems, how would you know you weren't talking to the actual one that had done it?"

"Hmmm." She pulled her other leg out of her coveralls and stepped clear of them. "I guess I wouldn't know. I'd just be careful, talk to someone that I'm sure has no connection to LifeLine. I'll try to stay out of trouble. . . ."

Steve studied her. "I don't know. I don't like the idea of you stepping on somebody's toes. If you ask the wrong guy, it could be dangerous. I still think you should let the NTSB complete its investigation. When that blood sample taken at the autopsy comes back showing CO poisoning—and you're convinced it will—Westover will have to change his mind, like it or not."

"Yeah, but that'll take three weeks, Steve! The person that caused the crash could be out of here within three weeks, easy, without even stirring any suspicion. He could get away scot-free, and I'm not going to let that happen."

"Why don't you just rely on the professionals to figure this out, Taylor? I think you're making too much of this carbon monoxide deal, and the rigged airstair bolts. If it was that obvious, the NTSB would've seen it, too. Just let it go."

"No, I can't do that. I owe it to Erica to clear her name—she wasn't at fault in this wreck."

"Are you positive of that, Taylor? Are you sure that you didn't make a mistake with her? Maybe cut her a little slack because you wanted her to succeed?"

Niggling doubts chewed on her subconscious, making her hesitate. Had she actually screwed up, without even realizing it? He could be right—after all, he *was* an uninvolved spectator.

Finally, she made a decision. "No, Steve, I'm sure I didn't make a mistake in signing Erica off. I think you know me well enough to see that I try really hard to keep my feelings out of things like that."

"Okay, as long as you're sure." He reached out and flicked her bangs off her forehead. "I just don't want you to bite off more than you can chew. Speaking of that, how about some dinner?"

She shook her head. "Naw, I'll take a rain check. I'm kind of tired." The truth was, Steve's comments about her view of Erica's pilot skills still bothered her. Maybe she'd have to do some more thinking that evening. Alone.

ELEVEN

Taylor turned over in bed without opening her eyes and reached out in front of her face, expecting to be squished up against the wall. Surprisingly, her hand connected with nothing but empty air, and she blinked in astonishment. She flipped over to see where Steve had wound up, thinking he must have learned some bed manners, only to realize that she had plenty of room because she was alone.

Oh, yeah. Now she remembered.

Sliding to the side of the bed, she hung over the edge and let the blood run to her head. She wondered if that made her think better. Even if it didn't, it altered the typical pattern of life for a few seconds, and that was a benefit. It was good to shake up the routine once in a while.

As she peered under the bed from her unusual position, she sighted a balled-up sock in the far corner. Wriggling closer to the edge of the mattress, she tried to reach for it, but no. It was too far away.

Undaunted, she hung halfway out of bed and felt around in the dust balls, stretching and stretching with no luck. Then, with a final jab, she connected with the sock, just as she slithered completely out of the covers and toppled head-first onto the floor.

"Oh, shit," she complained. Rolling over and sitting up, she examined the sock wad in her hand. "Hey, I was wondering where this went. I thought the dryer ate it." After stuffing her unexpected discovery into the hamper, she stood and glanced at the clock.

Guiltily, she read the glowing LED digits: 8:32 a.m. She wasn't even dressed yet—was she turning into a sloth, or what?

While she hastily donned her clothes—cords and a hefty cotton sweater in honor of the dismal-looking weather outside—she contemplated what she had to do that day. If she didn't get beeped for a medevac, she'd have the whole day to herself. She remembered her conversation with Steve the previous night. He had been a bit—a bit?—unsure of her conclusion to the accident, and her resolve to look into it, so she'd better justify her view by talking to a skilled mechanic herself. There was no point in pursuing her investigation if the fatal wreck couldn't have been planned.

Balanced on one leg, she slipped a sock over her toes and contemplated the situation. Who could she talk to?

Not one of LifeLine's own mechanics—even though they knew the King Air well, they were too close to the disaster on Mt. Iliamna. Steve was right about one point: she had to make sure she wasn't talking to the person who really *did* have knowledge of sabotage, because he'd done it.

But who else did she know in aircraft maintenance? It had to be someone far enough from LifeLine to be safe, but still someone that knew complex systems and would be willing to talk her.

Then it dawned on her: Isaac Kvalvik, a man she'd known during her days with Tundra Air Charter in Bethel. Even though he'd been employed by a competitor, the aviation community was small and everyone knew everyone else. From the grapevine she'd heard of his move to Anchorage, but where had he gone?

She padded over to the bedroom's phone and dialed LifeLine. After a minute of shooting the breeze with Colin Stuart, the mechanic on duty, she knew who had hired Isaac. One call later, she had an invitation to stop by his workplace to chat.

Once she'd cradled the phone, she climbed down the ladder from her sleeping quarters. As she shuffled down the rungs, she assured herself that she would build a proper stairway to the loft. Preferably before she fell off the ladder while negotiating it in the middle of the night.

When she reached the ground floor without any mishaps, she walked into the kitchen and prepared a bowl of hot cereal to calm her grumbling stomach.

Finishing her breakfast, she cleaned and dried the bowl, then started on solving another riddle. Where the hell were her car keys?

Pulling into the parking lot in front of the Alaska Air Network, she studied the building and sighed. She'd always wanted to work for the Net, but couldn't get them interested in hiring a neophyte pilot. Especially a *female* neophyte pilot.

By the time they joined the twentieth century and finally offered a job to a woman, she had already been working for LifeLine for three months. Oh well.

After maneuvering into a cramped parking slot and turning the ignition off, she clambered awkwardly out of her Suzuki. That was one of the problems with four-wheel-drive vehicles—you were always so high off the ground that no graceful way existed for climbing in or out of them. She zipped her flight jacket and ambled toward the big, red hangar-office complex.

Sidestepping an expectant receptionist ready with directions, she headed across the front lobby and pushed the door to the hangar open. Her eyes widened—the hangar view always impressed her, every time she visited.

Men rushed to and fro across the gleaming floor of the hangar, all clad in uniforms specific to their duties, like soldiers in the military. Mechanics working on DeHavilland Twin Otters or Convair 580s, wielding sparkling stainless steel tools, were dressed in crisp blue coveralls with company logos and name tags. The ramp attendants driving spotless aircraft tugs wore matching jackets and trousers, again with insignia displayed on their chests. Even the flight attendants stepping off one of the Convairs had their version of company outfits, fashionable and color-coordinated.

Trying not to stick out in the middle of so many busy figures, she strode toward the office where Isaac Kvalvik waited. She hoped that if she walked purposefully, sure where she wanted to go, she'd look like she belonged there, uniform or not.

Out of the corner of her eye, she spotted a King Air parked nearby. Good, the Net had at least one of those planes—undoubtedly Isaac had worked on it and knew enough to tell her if it could be tampered with.

Poking her head in the office, she saw Isaac and another mechanic leafing through a maintenance manual for one of the aircraft. He glanced up at her entrance, peered at her without any recall in his eyes, then grinned when it hit him a second later. "Taylor, I didn't recognize you! It's been ages!" he boomed in his deep baritone.

That had always surprised Taylor, his reverberant voice. It didn't seem to match his minimal height and New Age looks. Even though Isaac was a full-blooded Yup'ik Eskimo, very little about his appearance gave that away. A ponytail pulled his coarse, black hair back, and his tar-pit-dark eyes hid behind tinted spectacles. Only his flat nose and rounded face, and his short, stocky build, betrayed his Alaskan Native heritage. He extended a hand to shake hers.

"Boy, Isaac, it sure *has* been a while," she commented when his firm grip met hers. "What's it been, four years?

It looks like you've come up in the world, wrenching on Twin Otters and Convairs in a heated hangar. Sure beats freezing your balls off outside, trying to do a hundred-hour inspection on a Cessna.''

He laughed, then studied her intently for a moment. She felt a bit awkward—his gaze was piercing. "You're looking good, Taylor," he murmured. She couldn't help feeling as though he was looking at her as a woman, not a pilot.

"I'm looking good? Did I look all that bad in Bethel?" she joked, attempting to break the tension with levity.

"Oh, you know what I mean. You looked good in Bethel, too." He crossed his arms with a smile. "So, I hear you're driving for that upstart medevac company across the airport. How's it going?"

"Just fine, Isaac. Just fine." She nodded toward the door, a question in her eyes. "Can I talk to you outside for a sec?"

"Hey, sure." He turned to the other mechanic, who had gone back to the manual after scoping her out. "Hey, Rick, I'll be back in a flash. Come on, Taylor." He gestured at the door with a smile.

In the five seconds it took to walk back into the cavernous hangar, she contemplated how to approach Isaac with her questions. Should she just make up some story to cover her interest in the details of King Air systems? Or should she come clean with him, trust that he would listen to her and keep his mouth shut? She didn't want word of her investigation of the fatal wreck to circulate—the wrong person could hear of it.

Finally, she decided she had no choice, she'd have to tell Isaac the truth. After all, he was a major source of information, but more importantly, she felt she could trust him.

Shutting the door behind them, he swung around and looked up at her. At only five foot five, he had to tilt his head a tad to meet her eyes. "So, what's up? You said you had some King Air questions for me, but you were pretty vague on the phone.''

"Well, yeah. I've got a couple of questions about the oxygen system." She walked over to the Net's own King Air, parked near the door they had just exited through. With a sweep of her hand, she caressed the shiny paint on the aircraft's fuselage. "How easy is it to substitute some other gas for oxygen in the bottles that feed the masks? Could anybody do that? Can it be done at all?"

His eyebrows arched, expecting a more mundane question. "Oh, of course it can be done, it's easy. All you'd need is the equipment used to recharge the oxygen cylinders, and a source for the other gas. I don't know if the business that normally recharges the tanks would have the kind of gas you want, but I suppose they could find it." He folded his arms over his chest, appearing to enjoy being able to answer her question—it probably stoked his ego to have knowledge that the aircraft pilots didn't.

"But what if you didn't have the recharging equipment?" she asked. "What else could you use?"

"Hmmm, let me think." He gazed across the hangar at a group of three men who were struggling to replace a huge tire on one of the Convairs. He studied them for a moment, then turned back to Taylor. "Well, I guess if push came to shove you could use the same equipment made for filling scuba tanks. That'd probably work. Why do you ask, anyway?"

She ignored his question and tried another of her own. "One more thing, Isaac. If you sawed through the bolts on an airstair to make it fail, how could you bypass the circuits that warn of the seal rupturing?"

"Whoa, that's a weird thing to ask. You planning on doing that sometime in the future?" He laughed tentatively, obviously puzzled by what she was asking.

"Yeah, right." She laughed in turn, again ignoring his query. "How would you do that?"

He stared at her for a moment, appearing confused, before he shrugged and decided to answer her.

"Well," he said, "that'd be easy, too, if you knew something about the electrical system. Just solder the wires connected to the warning circuits to something else, and they're not going to alert you to anything.'' He appeared pleased with himself—the questions weren't all that difficult for a well-schooled mechanic.

She shook her head, thinking it seemed too easy. ''So all you need is some knowledge of the circuitry, huh? What if you don't know the King Air?''

''Just look in the maintenance manual—any mechanic knows how to follow a wiring diagram.'' Then he peered up at her, his curiosity getting the better of him. ''But why are you asking me about this stuff?''

''Well, uhhh . . .'' she stammered, realizing if she didn't tell him something, he was going to clam up. She needed a mechanic like him that she could talk to, so she decided to level with him. ''Did you hear about the King Air we lost a couple of days ago? The one that crashed on Iliamna?'' She felt her gut twist when she talked about the accident—she still wasn't over it. Perhaps that's why she had to find out what had happened; she needed to put some closure on the tragedy.

Isaac's eyes narrowed, and he stuffed his hands in his coverall pockets. ''Sure,'' he said cautiously, ''I heard about it. Everyone has. Is that what these questions are about?''

''Well, yeah, they are. I saw some odd things when I went down to the crash site, and I'm trying to figure them out. I wanted to run some scenarios past someone like you. But I hope you'll keep your mouth shut about talking to me, answering my questions. Can you do that?''

He nodded emphatically. ''It can be our secret, Taylor.''

She was glad that she'd chosen him—he obviously wanted to please her. She hadn't realized he'd be so easy to talk to until then—she rarely talked to him face-to-face in Bethel.

But it sure was working out for her now.

''Thanks for your help, Isaac. I'm glad I came to talk to

you. You're a sport.'' She gave him a quick peck on the cheek, not sure if that was necessary to ensure his further cooperation. She hoped it didn't feed the flames, give him the wrong idea of her gratitude. ''Anyway, I'll see you later.'' She swung around and headed across the hangar for the front lobby of the building.

With both hands poked into the front pockets of her cords, she shouldered her way through the door leading to the parking lot. It had been a very profitable trip, and she had just heard her theories given credence. But even though that's what she wanted, it raised the stakes—if someone had sabotaged LifeLine's King Air, he wouldn't be overjoyed to have his tampering discovered.

TWELVE

Right across Jewel Lake Road from the departure end of Runway Six-Left stood a sandy lot surrounded by a small park. Taylor Morgan pulled her Suzuki into it—she had a bit of thinking to do, and the roar of jets taking off seemed to help. It made her feel comfortable, in her own element.

The lot held several other cars, empty of people. Most likely, the drivers were somewhere nearby, on one of the trails that feathered from the fenced square. The park was a favorite location for exercising dogs. People went skijoring there during the winter—letting their excited huskies or setters tow them through the snow-filled woods on skis—and the fall months brought out black Labradors and agile terriers learning the art of duck retrieval. She had often stopped by here after completion of a medevac, entertained by the antics of the dogs and their humans.

The idea of a pet appealed to her, but her erratic schedule didn't really permit it. She was gone from home so often, and an animal was entitled to more attention from a human companion than she could offer.

Maybe she should just get a couple of goldfish.

Leaning back in her vehicle's seat, she entwined her fingers behind her head. Focusing on the cloth of the convertible top, she ruffled her bangs with a puff of air. What was the next question needing an answer in the King Air riddle?

Well, Isaac had let her know that sabotage was a possibility, but so what? She still didn't know who had done it.

The same fundamental enigma begged for a solution: Why would anybody want to bring a LifeLine aircraft down, resulting in the deaths of five innocent people? Was somebody trying to ruin the plane, sabotage the business, or kill somebody on board?

She pondered the riddle, dumbfounded by it. What could any of the people on board have done that would prompt a death threat? Not just a *threat*, but a successful attempt. She didn't know the flight nurses all that well, but they certainly didn't seem the type to get involved in activities that could provoke intimidation.

For that matter, she could say the same about Marshall Price and Erica Wolverton. The aircraft's captain had been a friend ever since Taylor had started with LifeLine, and he never impressed her as being a lowlife, nor did the companions she'd seen him with. She had little information about the younger woman, since she was so new, but Taylor got the same feeling from her.

Even the Yup'ik patient seemed a long shot for a premeditated killing. Granted, she'd heard of drug trafficking occurring in the villages, and the Native Alaskan man could have been a dealer targeted for a hit, but how could anyone have known he would be on that plane? It had to be something else, perhaps a plot to hurt LifeLine itself.

As she drummed her fingers on the steering wheel in thought, a thirty-something man and a golden retriever loped out of the woods and headed for a late-model Honda Accord. The young man had preppie written all over him, as did his dog—the human's state-of-the-art hiking boots were color-coordinated with his rain-repellent REI jacket, the canine had a bright red bandanna knotted around his neck as a collar. Mr. Yuppie waved at her as he climbed into the Accord, and Fido jumped right into the other seat as though he planned to drive from the wrong side of the car.

When the Honda pulled out onto Jewel Lake Road and turned south, a thought struck Taylor. She remembered the night of Erica's checkout flight in the King Air, when the two women had run into Cameron McNiven and his brother at the hotel bar. Just as the men were leaving, they were joined by Dave Kingsbury, the Learjet copilot LifeLine had to dismiss. His paranoid suspicion—that he couldn't find another pilot's job because Nate Mueller had blackballed him—rang in her ears. The words had sounded so vitriolic, so full of hate.

Could he have been angry enough at the office manager, and in effect at LifeLine, to have taken revenge by bringing a medevac flight down?

Of course, that was a rather drastic move—trying to tarnish LifeLine's reputation by sabotaging one of their aircraft, and ultimately killing five people—but she'd seen actions just as unbelievable on the TV news. It amazed her, the evil hatched by damaged, sick egos.

And that was worth checking into.

The Suzuki jumped to life as she keyed the ignition. After looking both ways for traffic, she pulled onto Jewel Lake Road and swung to the north, on her way to her employer's office. Maybe Cam was back from Seattle with the new King Air, and if he was, maybe he could enlighten her on his friend, Dave Kingsbury.

When she pulled into LifeLine's lot, she glanced at Erica Wolverton's aqua Geo. It looked so lonely there, all by itself, with no other cars surrounding it. Was it missing its owner? Taylor wondered, anthropomorphizing the vehicle.

She hiked across the parking lot toward the decal on the

front door of the office. The picture of Nate Mueller standing in front of the schedule board, a rag in his hands, filled the window. She pushed inside, with the hydraulic spring holding tension on the door swooshing as it swung closed.

"Is it raining yet, Taylor?" Nate asked without turning around. He lifted the cloth and erased DAY, printed on the line next to Todd Zemanek's name, and replaced it with NIGHT. Two arrows, one pointing left and one pointing right, encircled the NIGHT label and encompassed one week's time.

"Wow, Nate, you got eyes in the back of your head?" she quizzed him.

The office manager moved the towel to the line after her name and erased DAY there, too. "Naw, I saw you drive up," he said. He added OFF to her schedule, with arrows pointing at the next seven days. After surveying his work, he dropped the rag in a drawer and plopped into his chair. "So, what's up? I know you didn't get beeped. You just out killing time?"

"Yeah, I guess so." She wasn't about to tell Nate what she'd been doing—until she was one hundred percent sure she was on the right track, she had no intention of doing so. If she was wrong, he'd never let her live it down.

"So, is Cam back from Seattle?" She settled one hip onto the corner of his desk, the ubiquitous stack of papers on his blotter crinkling as she sat on them. "I want to take a look at the new King Air he brought back with Terry."

"Help yourself, it's in back." He pointed over his shoulder in the direction of the hangar.

"So it *is* here, huh?"

As she stood—shit, she really didn't want to see the new King Air, she just wanted to ask some questions—the front door opened again.

"Hi, guys, what's up?" Cameron McNiven entered the office and greeted Nate and Taylor with a grin. He was jauntily attired in a burgundy corduroy shirt and casual khaki slacks, his flight jacket tossed over one shoulder like an afterthought, a nautical-looking web belt encompassing his waist. Tasseled loafers—worn enough to look hip, but not enough to look grungy—peeked out from under the cuffs of his pants.

Damn, he's a natty dresser, she concluded, wishing she dressed as well. He certainly didn't look like he belonged in an airplane as anything but a flight attendant.

"So, Nate, you got that paint job set up? Are they ready for it?" he asked.

Leaning back in his chair, Nate nodded. "They'll take it this afternoon. You and Taylor can fight over who takes it across the field."

"What are you talking about?" she asked. "You mean the new King Air?"

"Yeah, we didn't get it repainted in company colors while we were in Seattle," Cam replied. "We couldn't find anybody that could take a rush job. Nate said come back anyway, he'd work something out here in Anchorage. And I guess he did." Shrugging into his flight jacket, he nodded at the hangar door. "You want to arm wrestle to see who'll taxi it over to South Airpark?"

"Well, why don't we both take it over, walk back? I could use a little exercise."

"Okay, I need to stretch my legs, too," he commented, flipping his jacket collar up in preparation to depart. Taylor figured he didn't do that because he expected it to be chilly outside, but because it looked so cool. Typical.

He cocked his head toward the hangar and gestured for Taylor to lead the way. "Ladies first," he said, bowing in exaggerated politeness.

"You mean, 'captains first.' I'm still your superior," she cracked back.

"Anchorage ground, November six-three-three-whiskey-golf, north ramp, taxi to South Airpark," Cam recited into the boom mike that nestled against his lips. His thumb slipped off his push-to-talk button, opening the frequency for the reply from the air traffic controller in the tower a half mile away.

"Six-three-three-whiskey-golf, Anchorage ground, taxi to South Airpark, cross six-left and report holding short of six-right."

"Three-whiskey-golf copies, hold short of six-right." Cam added power to start the King Air's departure from the asphalt ramp in front of the hangar. After glancing out the window on his left, he turned to face Taylor.

"This is neat." He grinned. "I think I could get used to this real quick."

"I wouldn't get too used to it, though, if I were you," she teased. "You sitting in the captain's seat and me sitting in the copilot's seat isn't going to happen too often." She had surrendered the left cockpit seat to Cam for the trip across the airport to the paint shop, figuring that would be an ideal time to talk to him about Dave Kingsbury. She didn't want distraction during the trip, but she didn't mind if *he* got bothered by things. That way he might not ask her why she was so interested in his friend. Maybe if he suspected why she was quizzing him about Dave, he'd clam up before he divulged any damaging information.

"So, I wanted to ask you a few questions, about your friend Dave Kingsbury." She tried to sound nonchalant, like the subject had just popped into her head. "I was thinking about when me and Erica ran into you guys at the bar the other night, and I remembered how mad Dave sounded when he said he couldn't find another flying job."

With one hand on the twin throttles, one hand on the control yoke, and both feet on the rudder pedals, Cam maneuvered around a nasty pothole in the taxiway. "Yeah, he *was* pretty pissed. Every time he gets juiced up, he starts complaining about 'how Nate screwed me.' It gets kinda old after a while. I can see why he's ticked off—I mean, that's gotta be embarrassing for a pilot to get stuck working in a fucking video store—but still . . ."

"I can appreciate you getting sick of his whining. If you

hear the same story, time and time again, it loses its color."
She studied the taxiway slipping past them for a moment
before she spoke again, casually. "Hey, do you think he'd
ever do anything to get back at Nate for 'blackballing' him?
Does he have a temper, have you ever seen him get violent
when he's mad?"

"Hmmm." Cam narrowed his gaze, then nodded his
head, not detecting anything odd about the question.
"Yeah, he is kinda hot-tempered. I remember a party we
went to at Goose Lake this spring, a lot of pilots were there.
Some guy from one of the air taxis at Lake Hood asked
him where he was working now. He must've known that
Dave got fired, you know how fast stuff like that travels
on the grapevine—"

"You're not kidding about that, it moves at warp speed
in the aviation world," Taylor muttered, shaking her head.
That was why she didn't want the story of her digging to
get around—if it did, the entire airport would know in
about two days.

"Anyway," he continued, "the air taxi guy was needling
Dave because he couldn't find another job. The whole story
seemed real funny to the guy, especially the part about the
video store." He reduced the aircraft's speed to allow a
small Cessna trainer to cross the taxiway in front of him,
and he glared at it. "Why don't those trainers go somewhere else? They don't belong at an international airport,
they should stay at Merrill Field, where the students and
the CFIs usually hang out. There's too much commercial
traffic here."

She attempted to keep the other pilot on track with the
story about Dave—it was getting interesting. "So, what did
he do about the guy who was bad-mouthing him?"

Cam laughed. "The more Dave drank, the more pissed
he got. Eventually, he decided to slash the tires on the guy's
truck." He chortled some more, enjoying his recall of the
day.

"Dave slashed the guy's tires? And you're laughing about it?"

"Well, yeah. It was a lot better than what he wanted to do earlier. At first, he wanted to go back to Lake Hood and pour sugar in the gas tanks of one of the planes at the guy's air taxi! We talked him out of that scheme, but he figured he had to do something. . . ."

"Sugar in the gas tanks, huh?" Her eyebrows arched. Dave had been willing to cause the crash of an air taxi plane, which would have been carrying several people and a pilot. Would he have been as willing to seek revenge for his firing by sabotaging a King Air on a medevac?

Breaking into her guarded thoughts, Cam asked the question she hoped he wouldn't. "Anyway, why are you asking about Dave?"

Just as he spoke, Taylor yelled, "Cam, watch out! You're supposed to hold short!" Blue and green stripes flashed past as an Alaska Airlines 727 roared by on Runway Six-Right, directly in front of them.

"Damn!" The startled man slammed his feet down on the rudder pedals, braking the forward motion of the plane. "Oh, shit! That was close!"

Dashed lines, indicating where any aircraft must hold short of an active runway, sat five feet behind the main wheels of the aircraft. Taylor looked over her shoulder to see them, and reached up to put the throttles in *beta* range so she could back away from them. The burst of adrenaline that had flooded into her body two seconds earlier was ebbing, and she snorted. "Well, Cam, your first stint in the captain's seat was not an unqualified success. Do you think you can get us across the airport without hitting any more airliners?"

Eyes rolling, cheeks flaming, he nodded, and activated his mike to tell the ground controller that he was holding short of six-right.

•   •   •

"I wasn't wrong about suspecting sabotage, Steve," were the first words that came out of Taylor's mouth when she phoned his house. With the receiver cradled between her chin and shoulder, she settled comfortably on one of her love seats, staring out her front window. A squirrel was in her front yard, busily chewing on a nut, and it balanced on a nearby tree branch. She watched its tiny furry hands turn the object over as it nibbled on one side, then the other. Her feet, cocooned in sheepskin lounging booties, dangled over the arm of the small sofa. The picture of the squirrel gnawing on the nut reminded her that it was nearing dinnertime and she hadn't eaten anything since breakfast.

But even though she was hungry, she felt good—her digging into the King Air accident had panned out and she was proud of herself.

"You've got something new, Taylor?" Steve queried. "You must've connected with somebody today. I'm curious about what you found."

"Today I discovered that my guess about the cause of the accident wasn't far-fetched. It *could've* been done. Not only that, I found out who could've done it." She leaned her head back on the sofa's arm and began the story of her talks with Isaac Kvalvik and Cameron McNiven.

"See?" she concluded. "Not only could the King Air be tampered with, Dave could've done it. He had access to the airplane and the maintenance manual, he could've figured things without any problem. Plus, he's already proven he was willing to kill somebody that pissed him off. What a crackpot!" She shivered, even though the cabin wasn't cold—the idea that anyone could cause the death of others was really scary, especially when the killer felt protecting his ego justified his actions.

The fact that she used to work with Dave Kingsbury was even scarier—she had never seen his hidden side, and hadn't used any caution on the occasions when interacting with him. Luckily, she hadn't had much contact with him, or opportunity to piss him off.

"Well, Taylor, that's kind of upsetting information. I have to admit it, I had your theory pegged wrong. I thought maybe you had signed Erica off before she was ready, and were subconsciously trying to cover it up by inventing a harebrained story. But I guess I was wrong."

"Okay, apology accepted, Mr. Derossett. If that really was an apology." She smiled, pleased by getting her point across. "Hey, I'm starving. If you're really sorry you hurt my feelings—and you should be—you can buy me dinner as expiation."

"Expiation? Where the hell did that word come from?"

"Hey, my mind is a wealth of knowledge," she chortled, secretly acknowledging that "expiation" came off her WORD OF THE DAY calendar.

THIRTEEN

Taylor stirred her oatmeal absentmindedly as she stared at Steve, who stood at the stove cooking a couple of eggs. As he flipped them over, his toast popped up, and he abandoned the frying pan for a moment to tend to the bread. The crusts were burnt in places, but he still buttered the blackened slices and slid them on his plate. The eggs snapped and sputtered in the background—they, too, were getting a bit dark.

"How can you stand toast like that, burned beyond recognition?" she asked, her eyes widening in amazement at his culinary laissez-faire attitude. "I always have to scrape the edges off when that happens."

"I like things crispy," he assured her matter-of-factly. Plopping his well-done eggs on top of his toast, he set his breakfast on the table. "I could ask you why you like that soggy oatmeal, too, if I was that nitpicky." He grinned at her and sat down.

She wasn't going to let him get away with that jab, so she put on her Mom voice to lecture him. "Well, young man, I've read that the fiber in oatmeal cuts way down on your chances of getting colon cancer. That's good, but all

I've heard about burnt things, like black toast, is that the scorched pieces are actually carcinogens themselves. Looks like my breakfast beats yours, hands down.''

"Yeah, well, mine tastes better.''

She shrugged—he was entitled to his own preferences in food, but she didn't understand why his health didn't concern him. If he took care of the Learjet like he took care of himself, he'd get fired, no question about it.

But she *could* say something in his favor—he certainly exercised enough. She was reminded of that every time she wrapped herself around him in bed. He had a set of abs you could bounce a quarter off—not to mention a butt worth taking a second mortgage on your house for—which greatly improved the esthetic qualities of their intimate play. That was one of the many qualities of their relationship she loved, and she couldn't fathom the fact that she almost didn't seize the opportunity to pursue him when they first met.

A relationship with another pilot wasn't what she had been looking for at that point in time, several years earlier. Her last close friendship with a pilot became difficult when professional rivalry began to pose problems, and she and her lover—who flew for a rival air taxi—found themselves attempting to outdo each other, trying to be the one who fought the weather the hardest or took the toughest cargo load. That one-upmanship would have killed them if they'd continued it.

But no need to spar had blossomed between her and Steve, probably because they worked for the same company, rather than competitors.

In their relationship, the fact that he was another pilot was only a benefit. They understood the way each other's heads worked, because their own heads worked in the same manner. They recognized the feast or famine quality of their jobs, and weren't upset when the other had to bow out of plans because of a medevac dispatch.

And it got even better—when you put two pilots in bed

together, the sparks were sure to fly. The personality traits that drew them to the command of a multimillion-dollar aircraft also made them daring and uninhibited between the sheets.

Spooning more oatmeal into her mouth, she allowed herself to relive the previous night's activities. She remembered the flurry of anticipation churning through her as he teased her and made her wait for her release.

They had outdone themselves—even though little time had passed since she'd enjoyed his attentions, the sex was always better after a short reprieve. Her eyebrows arched in recall, and the tingle in her crotch made her adjust her position on the chair.

"So, Taylor," Steve said, breaking into the enjoyment of her memories, "now that you know about Dave Kingsbury, don't you think you'd better tell somebody about it?"

She looked up, spoon poised in her oatmeal. "Like who? I can assure you that Westover wouldn't listen to me—he probably won't until I have pictures, or fingerprints, or something tangible." She examined the facts she had, sure she didn't have enough to interest him, or anyone else.

Then she frowned, wondering if she still had a duty to bring those facts to the NTSB investigator's attention, regardless of his interest.

Maybe she *should* say something.

"Okay," she acquiesced, "I'll go talk to him. I'm off this week, anyway, I may as well do something constructive. Make myself useful." She scooped up the last bit of oatmeal and stood from the table as she chewed it. "I'll take off in a few minutes," she mumbled, with her mouth full. She toted her bowl to the kitchen sink and splashed some water into it, saving the scrubbing for later.

After stepping away from the counter, she unbuttoned her Levi's and tucked her flannel shirt into them. "You think this'll be too warm for today?" she asked rhetorically. A glance out the kitchen window had shown her patches of gold amongst the birch trees in her backyard. Obviously, autumn was on its way, with the accompanying cooler days—at the higher elevations, fall came early.

She turned away from the window and looked across the kitchen, studying Steve's movements as he wiped up egg yolk with the last piece of his toast. "What's on the docket for you today?" she quizzed him.

"Oh, I've got to go into the office, update the Jepps for the Lear." He tossed the yolk-yellowed toast in his mouth and groaned. "That's an endless duty. As soon as I'm done with one set, the next one comes in."

"Yeah, I know what you mean." She walked across the living room to where her flight jacket hung from a peg near the door. Looking over her shoulder at him rinsing his breakfast plate, she grabbed the jacket and shoved an arm into a sleeve. "You ready to go?"

"Yeah, I guess so." He met her at the door, threw his own jacket over his denim shirt, and reached for the knob. "Good luck with Westover, okay?"

"Oh, yeah." She rolled her eyes, hoping he'd see how enthusiastic she was about driving over to the NTSB office and locking horns with a fed.

Once Steve had disappeared down her driveway in his Camaro—she wished he'd get rid of that car, get something less of a phallic symbol—she slammed the door of her Suzuki and keyed the ignition. *"rrrRRRRRR,"* it growled, and she squinted at it in annoyance. It was revving up too high when it started, cranking over to about three thousand RPMs. It had been doing that recently—probably needed a tune-up. She decided she'd suck up to Colin Stuart, the mechanic, next time she saw him at the hangar, plead with him to tinker with the idle setting. Maybe that would do it.

The racket of the engine startled a magpie, and it flapped off, its black-and-white coloring contrasting sharply with the day's gray monotony. She looked up at the ashen sky, hoping it would rain—she didn't really like rain, but *any* change in the dreary weather would be welcome. Not even the changing colors of the birch thickets could add enough to the day-in, day-out drabness of August.

Then again, she thought, it wasn't snowing.

She drove around the massive pine that served as the centerpiece of her circular driveway and set off down the bumpy path that led to the asphalt street two hundred feet away.

A brief glance showed her the street was clear of traffic, so she zipped around the corner at the end of her drive without stopping and headed downhill. Downtown Anchorage and the NTSB office were about eighteen miles away, and she had a promise to fulfill.

The trip down O'Malley Road would be uneventful; there weren't even any stop signs or lights to think about for a while. It was a straight shot down the steep thoroughfare for about five miles before she reached the Lake Otis Parkway crossing, and until she got there she'd have a chance to think, uninterrupted, about what she'd say to Westover.

She turned her radio on, tuned in KBFX, 100.5, and started tapping her fingers on the steering wheel. Mick Jagger and the Rolling Stones were belting out "Start Me Up," and she increased the volume to help her think. Strange how that worked, she thought—pumping up the volume pumped up the brain waves.

Pursing her lips and exhaling deeply, she examined her upcoming conversation with Westover. How should she approach him? she wondered. Should she be forceful, insist that he listen to her hunches—and that's all they were, anyway, just hunches—or should she act more deferential?

She hated the idea of imitating a numb-nuts for his benefit, acting like someone without much of a brain or a clue on how to use it. Yeccch . . . She shuddered.

The Alaska Zoo swept by as she continued her downhill roll. She glanced over and saw a group of children queuing up in front of the ticket booth—most likely they were a class from elementary school on a field trip. She could pick out the adult watchdogs hovering nearby, attempting to keep a handle on the kids while they paid for the tickets.

With the zoo disappearing behind her, she crested the last plateau before Lake Otis and moved her foot over to nestle next to the brake. The traffic light had just turned yellow; she planned to let the vehicle coast down the far side of the hill while the light was changing to red.

She moved her left foot up from the rest on the floor and grazed the brake pedal, tapping it to reduce her speed a fraction. The brake felt a little peculiar under her foot, kind of mushy.

Hmmm. That was odd.

Glancing at her speedometer, she realized the needle hadn't shown any decrease when she'd touched the pedal— if anything, she was accelerating as the hill's slope angled more steeply. She pressed a bit harder on the brake, but the vehicle continued to accelerate. Something was wrong.

A burst of adrenaline dispersed across her body, accompanied by a sharp intake of breath. She stared at Lake Otis, her eyes widening in horror—a constant stream of morning traffic clogged the crossing, the drivers heading for East Anchorage schools and offices. She was going to plow right through them.

Pumping the brake did nothing to the Suzuki's velocity, and even though it appeared the brakes had failed, she couldn't keep herself from repeatedly stamping on the pedal.

"Oh, shit!" she screamed, as the vehicle bore down on the cross-street traffic. She could feel the repercussive beat of her heart throbbing in her temples. *Wham-ba-Wham-ba-Wham!*

She stomped on the tread of the brake pedal frantically, screaming, "Get out of my way, get out of my way! I can't stop, I'm going to hit you!" The scene of impending disaster had her bleating at the cars senselessly, her words drowned by her hammering on the horn.

Honk, honk! HHHHHHoonnnkkk! HOOOONNNKKK!!!

Then her brain clicked over to another mode, survival mode, and she reached down to click the ignition off. But before she'd connected with the key, she heard her brain screaming at her from some faraway reach: "No, not the key! That won't help you, you gotta downshift to slow the car! Steer into the ditch!" Her many years of driving on the icy winter streets of Anchorage had taught her how to handle an out-of-control car—you never used the brakes to stop, but employed the gears, downshifting to a reduced speed. As a last resort, if you'd completely lost it, you aimed for one of the deep snow berms along the roadside and slowed the car by hitting it.

Of course, it wasn't winter and there weren't any drifts to plow into, but there *was* a shallow trench alongside O'Malley, full of brush, and that would work just as well.

With her breath rasping in her throat, she began punching the clutch with her foot as she manipulated the stick shift. She had to change gears, rapidly, to force the Suzuki to slow.

rrrRRRrrr! . . . The engine screamed as she downshifted from fifth to fourth at sixty-five miles per hour.

rrrRRRrrr! . . . It wailed again as she dragged the stick from fourth to third.

rrrRRRrrr! . . . third to second.

The engine continued to shriek as she cranked the stick down to first gear. She had made some progress in reducing her speed, but not slow enough, and not soon enough.

Her face twisted—the sound of the screaming engine was almost painful to hear, but she still hadn't brought the car to a stop. The needle on the tachometer was pegged on the red line when she wrenched the wheel to the side and headed for the shallow roadside channel.

The Suzuki leaped over the road's narrow shoulder and slammed into the bottom of the ditch, clods of dirt and torn tree limbs flying past the windshield as it rocketed downhill. It bounced from side to side as pings and scrapes filled the air, and rocks dislodged from the hardened earth bombarded its hood and grille.

Again and again she was thrown up against her seat belt, only the lap harness preventing her from smacking the roof and breaking her neck. As the car flattened bushes and shrubs with its passing, its speed finally began to diminish and movement of the steering wheel produced some response.

Even though the fire of the adrenaline rush still coursed through her system, Taylor was fairly sure she was going to make it out of the jam with nothing but a totaled car and a few nasty bruises.

That is, right before she saw a pile of rocks and boulders in front of her, the base for somebody's driveway that crossed the ditch at a ninety-degree angle.

"Oh, shitttt!" she yowled, as the vehicle plowed into the solid gravel wall. She was jettisoned against her seat belt, the shoulder harness pulling her short of a serious injury, but abrading her neck as her head snapped to the side. The sudden stop knocked the breath out of her—her vision grayed and became a tunnel, then flicked to black.

The next thing Taylor saw was a grandfatherly-looking man pounding on the driver's side window of her vehicle.

"Miss? Miss?! Are you okay?" he yelled, his eyes bugged out in excitement. His wide tie flapped from one side to the other as he jerked on the door latch, unable to wrench it open.

She shook her head to clear the colored, dancing bugs out of her eyes, and lifted a hand to show the frantic man outside that she wasn't dead. "I'm all right . . . I think," she murmured, not sure if the man could hear her faint croak.

In the near distance she saw a small crowd milling about, their cars lined up on the side of the road, two middle-aged men trotting toward the Suzuki from the group. The closest car, a Taurus station wagon, was likely owned by the gray-haired man trying to wedge the Suzuki's door open with a stick.

After gaining a bit more of her senses, she undid her belt and tried the inside latch. Nothing budged—it appeared hitting the dirt berm had bent the frame so the door wouldn't pop open.

Good thing nothing had caught on fire after the impact, she thought—she wouldn't have been able to leap out of the car to save herself.

The elderly man still thumped on the window, signaling her to roll it down so he could talk to her. Gingerly—her neck ached from whiplash, and an abrasion across her clavicle stung—she cranked it open.

"Are you all right? Are you all right?" squawked Pops.

"Don't move," cautioned one of the other men as he skidded to a stop next to the car. "You may have broken your back or something. We need to immobilize it."

She glanced up at him, one eyebrow raised quizzically. Her spine felt fine, what was he thinking of? Obviously, the guy watched *ER* on television and was sure he had witnessed a nearly fatal crash. She didn't hit the embankment *that* hard, though.

Rolling over onto her back, her head on the passenger's seat and her feet planted on the driver's-side door, she attempted to kick it open. Two somewhat light thuds, and one really hard stomp later, the jammed lock burst clear from the striker plate and the door whipped open, nearly flattening Pops's nose. She sat up, dropped her feet down to the bottom of the ditch and stood.

A smattering of applause rose from the small crowd when it appeared she was okay. She stared at them for a second, then raised her hand to acknowledge them. The ovation made her feel a lot like an Olympic medalist, succeeding against long odds. It kind of embarrassed her—she hadn't done anything extraordinary, she was just trying to save her own hide. But it was nice that they seemed to care.

As she stretched her limbs, checking for sprains, the two younger men asked if she needed any more help. When she shook her head they excused themselves and headed for their cars. Only Pops remained, peering down at her.

Scanning the Suzuki, she mumbled, "What a mess," and turned back to study the path she had just hoed through the ditch.

"You were going too fast, hon, you lost control and wound up in the ditch," the solemn man chastised her.

She raised her eyebrows. "No, I didn't just lose control and run off the road, I did it on purpose to stop the car. My brakes went out. If I hadn't done that, my car would've been in the front seat of your Taurus, rather than over here in the weeds." She swung around to look at her small four-wheel-drive vehicle again, disbelief in her expression. How did that happen, her brakes failing?

"They went out, huh? I hear they're having a special at Midas," he offered. "You ought to get them fixed."

"Well, it's kinda late for that, isn't it?" She sighed and walked to the front of the car. The grille was buried in the dirt bank. She wondered what the owners of the driveway would think when they discovered somebody had plowed into it.

Then her mind switched to here-and-now factors. "How the hell am I going to call for some help?" she wondered out loud. "It doesn't look like anyone is home at this house here."

Wordlessly, Pops reached into his suit jacket and handed her a cellular phone.

She stared at it, dumbfounded. *This guy isn't too old-fashioned, is he?* she acknowledged. Nodding gratefully, she thanked him and grabbed it. In a minute, she had Steve on the line and was telling him about the "strangest thing that just happened."

FOURTEEN

"Taylor! Taylor, are you okay?" A hand touched her thigh gingerly. She saw the size of the fingers behind the gentle caress, and knew exactly who it was.

"Yeah, I am, Steve," she said, her voice muffled. "I'm a bit sore, but it looks like I've got other things to worry about." She was sprawled underneath her Suzuki, her head hidden by the chassis, her legs poking out between some crushed bushes.

Dragging herself out from under the vehicle, she stood and began brushing twigs and pebbles from the seat of her Levi's. With every swipe, a cloud of dust rose. "I think I've got a real problem here," she said with emotion.

"Yeah, I'd say so," he replied.

Something odd about his tone of voice prompted her to glance up, and the image she saw caught her off-guard—his shoulders quivered, and he held a hand up to cover his mouth. He was laughing.

She straightened up immediately and looked at him, arms akimbo. "What the hell's the joke?" she quizzed him, not sure why he found her predicament humorous. "I could've been killed if I hadn't been able to stop—I don't find that too funny."

"Well, in retrospect, it *is* pretty funny, your four-by winding up waist-deep in the pucker brush. I was really worried that you were hurt, but now that I know you're okay I can laugh." He shook his head, still grinning. "I knew it'd catch up with you, the way you tear around in that car of yours. Actually, I thought you'd roll it some-day—I told you when you got it that those rigs were really unstable, with that short wheelbase and high center of grav-ity."

An old half-ton Ford truck roared by on O'Malley, its lack of a muffler producing an obnoxious racket. Steve swiveled to scowl at it, then returned his gaze to her. "I guess now that you've totaled the Suzuki, you can get something more stable, something that can handle the way you drive. Something closer to the ground." He crossed his arms across his chest and surveyed the damage to the ve-hicle, as well as the furrow her car had dug in the ground. "You don't do anything halfway, do you?"

"Hey, it was someone else who did this, it wasn't my fault!" She waved angrily at her vehicle, really pissed. Not only was her *car* totaled, it appeared *she* was supposed to get totaled with it. "The fucking brakes went out on me! Take a look yourself: the brake bleeder valves are loose, there's no fluid in the line! Bleeder valves don't loosen on their own, somebody worked on them!"

His gaze narrowed, then he dropped to his knees to peer at the car's undercarriage. Reaching underneath the chassis, he ran his index finger over one of the brake lines, and when he pulled it back, a drop of clear fluid glistened on the end. "Damn, you're right. It's all leaked out." He struggled to his feet and studied her indignant expression.

"I would've been dog meat if I hadn't been thinking on my feet," she growled. "Hitting that berm was bad news, but it would've been a lot worse if I *hadn't* hit it. Lake Otis was full of traffic, and I would've taken half of those cars with me!'' She stuffed her hands in her jeans' pockets, still glaring.

He leveled his gaze on the battered Suzuki, then looked over at her. "But who did this, who tampered with the brakes? You got any guesses?''

"That's pretty obvious, isn't it? It had to be Dave Kingsbury, no doubt about it. One day after I get some dirt on him, my car gets sabotaged and I'm almost killed in the process. You think those two events aren't related?'' She looked at him sideways, rubbing the abrasion at the base of her neck. "One way or the other, that sabotage was meant to shut me up. Either he wanted to scare me off, or he wanted to kill me. And he's shown that he has the kind of warped mentality that could justify doing something like that.''

She stopped talking for a moment, the anger in her eyes being replaced by worry. "I guess you *were* right, I need to talk to somebody about this. It's even more important now, and Westover needs to hear about Dave's connection to the King Air accident. Maybe I'll tell Trooper Hall about my brakes, too. We're talking homicide now.''

Withdrawing her hand from her neck, she headed for Steve's Camaro and resumed brushing the dirt and twigs off her pants. Once she reached the car, she grabbed the door latch and looked over her shoulder. "Hey, can I borrow this? I need some wheels. I'll come back to get the Suzuki later, but I need something right now for the trip to the NTSB.'' Without waiting for an answer from him, she opened the door and dropped into the passenger's seat.

"Hey, wait a second!'' he yelled after her; then walked to the car and climbed in. "I'm on duty today, I need my car if I get beeped.''

"Oh.'' She fastened her belt and thought for a bit. "Well, I guess I'll have to get Nate's rig. He'll probably let me use it.''

Steve nodded, then reached to start the car. Before he keyed the ignition, he turned to her with a question in his eyes. "How do you think Kingsbury found out you were asking about him? Do you figure Cam told him? He was the only one except me that knew about it."

"Yeah, you're right." Her face contorted, the skin on her forehead wrinkling. "I thought I had been pretty good at making it sound kind of innocuous when I talked to Cam, but maybe he picked up on it later." She glanced out the window, then turned back to face Steve. "He must've called Dave right after he left the hangar. I was with him all of the rest of the time; he couldn't have done it then."

With her lips pursed, she stared at her feet; "But what if Cam didn't tell Dave, what then? If Dave didn't even know I was checking up on him, he couldn't have been the one that worked my brakes over. Damn, this doesn't really make any sense." Then she gestured at O'Malley Road in a dismissive manner. "Well, whatever. Let's just head for the hangar. Maybe Cam'll be there and I'll figure out if he told Dave anything. Either way, I still need to get a hold of a car."

During the twenty-minute drive back to LifeLine, she was quiet, busy examining the brake-failure incident. Was she making it seem more sinister than it really was? Maybe Suzuki Sidekicks had a reputation for having brake problems. After all, she'd bought it used, and had had it for two years—no way of knowing what kind of care the former owner gave it.

But regardless of the amount of attention the vehicle got, something was fishy about losing the brakes. She turned away from the window. "You know, bleeder valves just don't work their way open after a while. I don't think I'm making this sabotage thing up. Somebody *did* tamper with my car."

"Hey, I believe you, Taylor, you don't have to convince me." He switched his concentration from the road to her. "I think you've got a real problem. That's one of the reasons why I didn't want you to start sticking your nose into things to begin with." He stared at her pointedly.

"Well, now that I'm in the thick of things, I'm not going to quit. Nobody's going to blame Erica for the King Air accident—*now* I'm sure someone else was responsible for it. In light of that job on my brakes, I'd say Dave's the one, and he must be getting a little nervous right now." She crossed her arms across her chest, her body language announcing that she refused to change her mind about it.

Steve shook his head, concerned. "What are you going to do if you find out that Cam didn't say diddly-squat to Dave, that there wasn't any way that he could've been the one that worked on your brakes?" He studied her, then turned back to watch the road. "Are you going to give up then?"

"That remains to be seen. I haven't talked to Cam yet, so don't count Dave out until then."

Turning to gaze out the window at the stores lining Dimond Boulevard, she noted the cars filling their parking lots. A retailing explosion had swept over South Anchorage—a plethora of variety stores like K-Mart were attempting to draw customers from the more established small boutiques in the large Dimond Center mall. She didn't know what the discount giants saw that she didn't see, but Anchorage was a happening place in a lot of expansion plans.

She broke away from the sights around her and spent the next several miles examining the most recent riddle: What *would* she do if it appeared Dave Kingsbury had no involvement in the morning's accident? Somebody had tampered with her brakes, but who?

Her life might be connected to the solution to that mystery.

FIFTEEN

Five minutes later, when Steve pulled into the LifeLine lot, Taylor was at the bottom of the rather short list of people with links to both the King Air accident and the sabotage of her Suzuki. Sighing, she turned to him and gestured at a rusty, dented Honda parked near the office. "I guess I'll talk to Nate, see if I can take his piece of junk." She climbed out of the Camaro and headed for the building, gesturing for him to follow. He stayed in the car, informing her that he had to get his flight case repacked before he came in.

She shrugged and walked away. Upon pushing the glass door open, she was greeted by a surprised Nate Mueller. "What are you doing here? It's your week off."

"Yeah, I know, but I have to borrow a car. Can I use yours? I won't need it for too long."

Her coworker grinned at her. "You can borrow it, as long as you don't mind not getting where you want to go. One of the CV joints on it is nearly shot, and when it gives up the car won't do anything but sit and spin its wheels. That wouldn't be a problem, would it?" he deadpanned.

"Yeah, right. I'm not a big fan of hitchhiking; I think I'll pass."

"Why do you need a car, anyway? What's wrong with your Suzuki?"

"I had a little trouble with it this morning, but I don't have time to talk about it now. Ask Steve about it when he comes in; he's outside fussing with his flight case. Anyway, where am I gonna get some wheels?"

Nate peered out the window and scanned the parking lot. Pointing, he said, "Why don't you take Erica's Geo? Her dad said you could use it—didn't you say he nearly *begged* you to use it?"

Glancing over her shoulder, she focused on the compact vehicle and shuddered. She couldn't take Erica's car; she could barely make herself look at it.

But where was she going to get another car? She had to get down to the NTSB, talk to Westover, tell him about what she had discovered and what had just happened. He couldn't deny it was important information.

Steeling herself, she walked over to the Peg-Board on the wall where several pairs of keys hung. She stared at them.

I'm sorry, Erica, she apologized soundlessly, *I have to have a car.*

"These are the keys to the Geo, right?" she asked rhetorically. A collection of silver keys dangled from a rawhide shoelace strung with native trade beads, and she ran her fingers over the attractive, colorful, and ethnic-looking piece. The previous summer she'd admired a similar set— key fob and matching necklace—in an Alaskan arts-and-crafts shop downtown.

She paused, then reached out and snagged the keys. Making a funny murmur, she turned and marched purposefully to the front door. Nate looked at her, confused by her odd expression, but said nothing.

When she headed toward the Geo, Steve called out at her from across the lot. "Hey, are you taking Erica's car?"

he questioned, somewhat nonplussed. He knew how looking at the dead woman's belongings unnerved Taylor.

"Yeah," she grunted. "I guess I am. No choice."

Applying the keys to the tiny vehicle's lock, she swung
the door open. The interior smelled a bit musty, perhaps
from the hamburger wrapper left to decompose by the shift
lever. She slid into the driver's seat, and paused. It felt
curious, lowering herself onto the vinyl upholstery, knowing who used to sit there. Kinda creepy.

The seat was positioned a bit farther from the accelerator
and steering wheel than it was in the Suzuki, for obvious
reasons—Erica had been a tall woman. Likewise, the
sleeves on her flight jacket, which dangled from the passenger's seat back, were long, too.

Taylor pulled the jacket to herself, forcing herself to hold
it. She'd have to take it back into the office and find a box
for it—when she went to Fairbanks for the memorial service she'd give it to Erica's folks.

When she laid the jacket back on the passenger seat, she
heard a crinkly noise in the pocket. Must be another burger
wrapper, she thought, and reached in to extract it.

However, the object she withdrew from the jacket pocket
was not what she expected. It was a crumpled photo, a
three-by-five print of a woman perched on a large, flat boul-
der that lay partially submerged on a stretch of beach. The
sandy ground was made up of flattened rocks, obviously
washed by the surf of some large body of water.

An ocean? she conjectured. A really big lake? Prince
William Sound?

Even as those thoughts flashed across her mind, she
smoothed out the wadded-up photo, and the most curious
part of the picture leaped up at her: the woman didn't have
a face. Someone had cut part of the print off, leaving her
headless.

What? Why would anybody deface a perfectly good por-
trait? she wondered.

She studied the photo intently, without spotting any clues

to why it had been cropped thus. Not until she flipped it
over and concentrated on some writing on its reverse did it
make sense. When she focused on the printing there, the
blood rushed from her face.

In precise penmanship, all the words capitalized, it said,
"I CAN CUT YOU IN, OR I CAN CUT YOU OUT. IT'S
YOUR CHOICE." The word *out* had been underlined numerous times, followed by exclamation marks. The threat
hadn't been casual.

Who was the note aimed at? she pondered, as she turned
the photo over again. Peering at it, she pored over the obviously female form, looking for details to the woman's
identity.

The stranger wore snug-fitting dark pants, made out of a
shiny material with the look of an odd texture to it. Vinyl?
she speculated. Stretchy vinyl? She'd never heard of that.
The pants seemed like something a rubber fetishist would
wear.

On the upper half of the woman's slender body clung a
polypropylene tank top, the erect nipples of her small
breasts protruding from the fabric. With no landmarks in
the background, it was hard to discern her height, and even
though Taylor scanned the photo thoroughly, she couldn't
tell who it was.

Was it Erica? she guessed. Or a friend of hers?

She squinted at the snapshot until her eyes watered, but
nothing indicated who had posed for it. Then her gaze froze
as she looked at the woman's throat and focused on the
necklace encircling the elegant, swanlike neck.

Dropping the photo, she retrieved the key fob from
where it hung on the Geo's ignition. She held it up against
the photo, comparing it to the necklace pictured there—the
two pieces matched.

Sucking in a breath, she lifted her face and stared blankly
out the windshield. *Erica* was the woman in the photo; the
threat had been aimed at her.

No wonder the King Air had gone down—somebody had

sabotaged it in order to get rid of the young copilot. She must have decided not to get involved in somebody's scheme, certainly thinking the person behind the threat didn't have the guts to stand by it.

But she had been *dead* wrong about that.

Then Taylor started. If the aircraft sabotage had been planned as a murder, the photo she held was evidence in a homicide. She shifted her grip on the snapshot to her fingertips, hoping to avoid smudging any prints on it. Glancing about the car, she realized the Geo might be evidence, too—if she took it, she'd have to be careful, wear gloves or something.

She vaulted from the Geo, photo dangling from her fingertips, and dashed to the LifeLine office. She had to tell Steve, let him know the situation was much more serious than even *she* had thought. When she burst through the front door, he was perched on the corner of Nate's desk, talking. He swiveled, startled by her pell-mell rush into the room. "Taylor, what the hell—"

"I've got it figured out, Steve, I've got it figured out! Erica is the hinge-pin! The King Air was sabotaged to—"

Then she stifled herself, realizing that he may not have told his coworker much of the story of her investigation into the accident. She wasn't sure how much Nate knew, and she didn't have time to tell him the whole story.

Steve seemed to know what she was thinking. "Nate knows everything. I filled him in. And he agrees with me, you should let the NTSB take care of it, they're the experts. If someone is willing to harm you to shut you up, it's time to step back." He repositioned himself on the desk, then focused on her blanched face. "Anyway, what were you yelping about when you ran in?"

She was sure he and Nate had been discussing how to get her to cool her heels, abandon looking into the fatal wreck. He surely thought she'd already gotten herself into enough trouble, what with the Suzuki brake problem and its meaning—not even *he* could deny that the fluid leak had been calculated sabotage.

She glanced at the photo between her fingertips, and gulped. If she told them much more of her theory, not only would she have Steve pressuring her to quit the investigation, Nate would be backing him up. But after weighing both sides of the argument for telling them, she decided she would. Even if they ganged up on her with admonitions to mind her own business, there wasn't any way they could force her to do so.

After glancing at Steve, then Nate, she waggled her index finger at the photo, careful not to touch it. "Well . . ." she muttered, "I found this photo in Erica's car." She steeled her resolve to hold her ground, and began to divulge what she thought the snapshot represented.

When she was done, she summed things up. "So it wasn't Dave Kingsbury that was behind the tampering on the King Air. I'm sure that whoever manufactured the accident meant it to kill Erica, and he didn't even *know* her. It has to be somebody else."

Steve's gaze narrowed. "I hate to encourage you, Taylor, but you may be right. What do you think, Nate?"

His coworker leaned forward in his chair, a grave expression on his face. "You *are* going to take this to Westover, right? The whole King Air deal is getting pretty serious now. I mean, we're talking murder here."

"Yes, I know. That's why I needed a car, to drive down to the NTSB office." She glanced at her watch, then reached for the phone. "Give me Westover's card. I'd better call him before I go down there. It's kind of close to lunch; he might have gone out."

After Nate handed her the investigator's card, she peered at the writing below the name. As she squinted at the tiny numbers, Steve's pager chirped at him, startling everyone in the room. "Well, that's convenient, catching me at the office." He laughed and glanced at the digital readout. "Ah, yes, hospital operations."

Nate lifted the phone receiver and dialed before holding it out to the other man. For a minute or so, Steve conversed with the dispatcher to get his assignment. "Okay . . . okay, yeah, I can handle that. . . . Okay, call Kai, tell him I'm already waiting for him at the airport. . . . All right. . . . Later, Shawna." He cradled the phone and glanced at Taylor.

"I guess you'll have to tell me about your visit to Westover when I get back." When she nodded, he turned to Nate. "They've got an ICU patient in a hospital in Corpus Christi who got hurt during his fishing vacation. The guy wants to get back to Anchorage for his recovery, be home with his family, so the Texan hospital called Cook Inlet to find out who they used to transport patients. Cook Inlet called us, so it looks like I get to fly down and pick this guy up." An airliner taking off from nearby Runway Six-Left rattled the windows, interrupting Steve and drawing his attention for a moment.

"Anyway," he continued when the noise subsided, "I'd better get the Lear ready to go. Kai'll be coming in right away—tell him I've started his preflight. I'll see you later." Jumping off the desk, he turned toward Taylor. "You be careful, you hear? Behave yourself at the NTSB."

"Yes, Mom." She watched him go, a bit disappointed that she couldn't talk to him after her trip to Westover's office, but also relieved that he wouldn't be challenging her on her look into the King Air accident for a while. She realized he was just looking out for her, but obviously he didn't see how important it was for her to put this puzzle together.

Sighing—she had no idea how the investigator would take her story—she grabbed the phone and dialed the NTSB. After two rings a pleasant voice answered.

"Anchorage field office," a young-sounding woman chirped.

"Investigator Westover, please."

"I'm sorry, but Mr. Westover has gone to Bethel to

cover an accident. We expect him back the day after to-morrow. Would you like to leave a message?''

Taylor groaned. She finally had some credible news to show him, and he wasn't even in Anchorage. Shit.

''No, no message,'' she said and cradled the phone. She stared at the photo on the desk and wondered what to do next. Then it dawned on her.

SIXTEEN

By the middle of the afternoon, Taylor was puttering down the Glenn Highway in Erica's Geo Metro, north-bound to the town of Wasilla. The younger woman had mentioned living there before the job offer from LifeLine prompted her to move back to Anchorage, so Taylor figured that would be her first stop in checking into the copilot's life.

When she had asked Nate Mueller for a look at Erica's job application—under the pretense of forgetting the names of the other woman's parents—she found the address and phone number she needed.

Not wanting any flak from him concerning her continuing search—he probably assumed she'd put it on hold until she could talk to Westover—she called the Wasilla number from a pay phone down the road and talked to the woman who owned the house. Jonquil Norback agreed to talk to her that afternoon, as long as Taylor arrived in Wasilla before four p.m.

"Give me plenty of time to get out of the house and on my way to work, okay?" requested Erica's former landlord after giving out directions to her home. "I have to supervise the waitresses on the evening shift, so I can't be late.''

''No problem, Ms. Norback,'' replied Taylor. ''I just have a few questions; it won't take much time at all.''

After replacing the receiver, she exited the phone booth and crawled back into the Geo. She didn't know how Erica had gotten her lanky body into the tiny car, but it must have been a tight fit. *Her* vehicle was similarly compact, so the aqua car was no big change for Taylor, but undoubtedly the tall woman had to make some sacrifices in comfort in the name of good gas mileage.

By the time she'd passed Eagle River, thirteen miles from the Anchorage city limits, Taylor's mind was fixed on the primary question in the riddle: Who would want Erica dead? And why?

Immediately an answer flashed across her consciousness, when she remembered that one of the first suspects in a murder investigation usually was a spouse. Especially an estranged spouse. That meant Erica's soon-to-be-ex-husband, the man who had rushed into the LifeLine hangar heaping abuse on Taylor a few days earlier. Could he have wanted his wife dead bad enough to sabotage a King Air to do it, if it meant killing four other innocent people in the process?

And was the ominous note she'd found in the young copilot's flight jacket also the work of the husband? Maybe she'd find something incriminating at Erica's old residence: a letter from one to the other, household paperwork they'd both signed, a credit card receipt.

Tapping her fingers on the steering wheel, she squinted at the asphalt slipping past her. The puzzle was getting more twisted with every discovery she made.

A late-model Eagle Talon, bright red, broke her concentration when it flew past her, doing about ninety in the left lane of the four-lane divided highway. Jerk, she thought, and gripped the steering wheel tightly. Wait until wintertime, pal, see how driving like that works on the icy roads.

She turned her thoughts back to the immediate problem

facing her and focused more intently on it. What could Erica have had on her husband that could elicit a death threat? Was that why she planned to divorce him, because he had concocted an illegal scheme that required her involvement?

As she pondered the possibilities, the picture of Erica's distraught husband filled her mind's eye. When he had barreled into the hangar screaming, blaming her for his wife's untimely end, he had seemed beside himself. If he was the one that actually *had* caused his spouse's death, how could he fake grief so genuinely? He had to be a consummate actor to pull that off—he certainly had fooled her.

Was his acting part of a plot to distract those looking at him as a suspect? Did he think they would not question a grieving widower crazed by a loved one's death?

Well, it wouldn't work with her. She'd ask some pointed questions of Jonquil Norback, see if Erica's former landlord had any information that could be useful to her, that could lead to a solution to the riddle.

Satisfied that she'd begun to follow a productive line of investigation, she turned back to admiring the terrain around her. Sleuthing was hard mental work, that was for sure, and she could use a break from it.

The trip up the Glenn Highway was always pleasant, with the craggy peaks of the Chugach Range bordering it on one side, the silty waters of Cook Inlet's Knik Arm flowing past it on the other. On a good day one could see the 20,320-foot Mt. McKinley rising from the distant horizon.

As she sped past the small native village of Eklutna, nestled in the trees next to the highway, she could see the spires of a Russian Orthodox church poking through the spruce crowns. A cemetery, half-hidden behind the branches, added a splash of color with its unusually bright grave markers. That form of religion, left by the Russian fur traders who visited the Alaskan natives of Eklutna decades ago, had lived on when they returned to their mother country.

Ten miles ahead of her stood the Butte, a tall, rounded knoll that seemed to guard the fertile soil of the Matanuska Valley. The floodplain of the Mat Valley, the hotbed of farming in Alaska, was famous for the enormous crops grown there. Every year at the State Fair those gigantic vegetables stood in state—ninety-seven-pound cabbages, zucchini squashes the length and breadth of a human arm, pumpkins so heavy they had to be moved by wheelbarrows. The greens owed their mammoth size to growing in the silty runoff of the Matanuska River, and the nearly twenty-four hours of sunlight dappling the Alaskan summer days.

She could still taste the sweetness of the juice she made at home from the immense Mat Valley carrots—two of the giants could produce enough flavorful nectar to fill a beer mug to its brim.

The memories of the delectable juice made her realize she hadn't had any lunch, and she wished there was some kind of fast-food joint between Anchorage and Wasilla. However, there wasn't even a McDonald's, so she'd have to put up with a cranky stomach for a while.

The bridges across the Knik and Matanuska rivers lay directly ahead, and as she rumbled over the first bridge, her mind focused on the dreadful secrets they had kept. The banks held the graves of more than fifteen women, strangled by a man who lured them to their deaths with invitations for an airplane ride. His vengeful quest to rid the world of women with *loose morals* would have continued but for the resourceful victim able to escape his clutches and contact the police.

By the time she turned left, off the Glenn Highway and onto the Parks Highway, she had erased those tragic images of death from her head and began looking forward to her chat with Jonquil Norback. Maybe she'd make another important discovery, now that she knew that Erica was a focal point in the investigation.

After passing the small vacant airfield in the center of Wasilla, she turned to her right and into the trees. Entire birch thickets sported gold leaves there—fall had progressed further in the small town than in Anchorage, due to its more northerly latitude. The nearby houses were set back from the road, cocooned in stands of evergreens that offered protection from the blasts of cold winter wind.

A mile further down the tree-lined road she glimpsed the house she was looking for. Jonquil Norback had told the truth when she said the house was hard to spot from the street—the small cedar-sided bungalow blended well with the trees, almost as though purposefully camouflaged.

The architectural interest of its shape minimized the house's lack of stature—a glassed-in segment stood nearest to the road, and angular extensions to the body added surprising variety to the structure. Obviously, someone had slaved long and hard in creating the design.

Pulling into the narrow driveway, she scanned the surroundings, wondering if she needed to watch out for moose there, since the woods were so close. Satisfied by her obvious safety, she stepped out of the car. Once she'd determined that she was not late—it was only 3:15—she rapped on the front door. A minute later, she knocked again, but still no answer.

She peered at her watch, concerned that it had stopped working. Was it actually past four and Jonquil Norback had left for work? The minute and second hands on her Seiko still moved, but she didn't have any other clocks to compare the time to. No bank time-and-temperature displays in the middle of the forest.

Just as she turned to head back to the Geo, disappointment wrinkling her features, the sound of gravel crunching under feet prompted her to glance over her shoulder. A slender, dark-haired woman wearing a burgundy jogging suit and expensive running shoes trotted into the yard from a path in the trees. She blew out a breath that ruffled her shaggy, blunt-cut bangs and dragged a hand over her fore-head.

"You Taylor Morgan?" she asked in a breathy voice. Her face-to-face voice contrasted a great deal with the one she used on the phone—maybe the former was meant to carry more authority, and she didn't feel she needed that when body language and gestures helped in getting her points across.

"Yeah, guilty as charged," Taylor quipped. "You must be Jonquil Norback." She studied the other woman per-functorily—the brunette seemed to be similar to her in age, height, and build, but the big difference between them was their chosen form of exercise. *She* hadn't jogged a day in her life, preferring stationary weight training to the joint-pounding of running. Her knees had never been good enough for that kind of abuse. "I was just getting ready to leave when you ran up. I'm glad we caught each other," she commented.

Jonquil collapsed on a patch of grass and began stretch-ing. "Yeah, me, too. I thought I'd have a few minutes for a quick run before you got here, but you made better time than I thought you would." She glanced at the Geo parked nearby, then regained her feet and bent to stretch her obliques.

When Jonquil's position bared her abdomen, Taylor no-ticed an odd belt around the other woman's waist. "What's that you're wearing?" she asked. "It looks like an ammo belt. You got bear problems around here?" She chuckled, hoping Jonquil would see the humor in her jest and realize she knew what the belt was for.

"Oh, this." The runner blushed furiously. "Erica didn't take this with her when she moved out. I was trying to get it back to her, but then . . ." She peered at her feet for a second or two, then shook her head and raised it. "But then she died in that accident. I guess she won't need it now; I don't think they do any scuba-diving on the other side. She probably won't need her computer, either, or any of the other stuff she left here. I've got it all packed up.''

"I didn't know Erica was a diver," Taylor commented. "I mean, she obviously was since she had a weight belt, but she hadn't mentioned it to me." She reached out and hefted the bulky belt, appreciating Jonquil's determination to exercise hard. "Anyway, can we go inside? I've got a few questions for you."

"Okay, come on in." Jonquil gestured for Taylor to follow her into the house.

SEVENTEEN

"Let's sit at the dinner table." Jonquil waved at a chair across from the one she dropped into.

Taylor chose a stool by the wall, and scanned the interior of the bungalow as she adjusted her position on the padded seat. Nubby-weave jute rugs covered nearly the entire first floor of the house with the wood flooring peeking out from beneath them here and there. A compact kitchen stood directly across from the dinner table, and elegant green plants hung from every corner, forming a foliage-curtain in front of upper-level sleeping quarters.

The living shield seemed like a good idea to her—maybe she'd try it at her own cabin. Hang some rhododendron and ivy from the peak of the A-frame's roof, let them dangle down to the lip of the loft.

The *zzziippp* of Velcro fasteners being loosened filled the room as the other woman pulled a sneaker off. "So, Taylor, you told me on the phone that you worked with Erica at her new job. But why are you asking questions about her? Are you investigating something?"

"Well, yeah, I guess I am. The NTSB, the National Transportation Safety Board, is looking into the accident she was killed in, but I don't think their conclusion to the cause of it is correct. I'm trying to find out what *really* happened.''

"The NTSB, huh? I figured they'd look into it. My brother Tommy's a pilot and he's always talking about them investigating crashes. What did they decide on, and why do you think they're wrong?''

"They're trying to pin it on Erica.'' Taylor caught Jonquil's incredulous look, so she gave her some more details. "They think that her captain was having a heart attack, and that she got so distracted by his trouble she lost track of things and flew the plane into the side of Mt. Iliamna.''

"Oh, bullshit!'' the dark-haired woman protested. "She wouldn't have done that! Tommy has flown with her—they worked together at Central Express—and he always said that she was a good pilot. No way was she responsible for that wreck!''

"Yeah, I agree. That's why I'm out here talking to you. Can I get your help?''

"You bet! What do you want to know?''

She pursed her lips, and glanced out a nearby window at the small garden in the backyard. All of the vegetables in it had been plucked from their stalks or vines—the remaining greenery was a bit wilted and blackened. She turned back to Jonquil with a question. "I know Erica was separated from her husband. Did she have a boyfriend?''

The slim woman raised an eyebrow slyly. "Well, I think she did, but I couldn't get her to talk about him. I think she might have been hiding the relationship, because of the pending divorce. If it got out that she was seeing someone else before she was officially single again, her husband would have had something to use against her in the proceedings. He could say she was an adulterer, that she'd been seeing the boyfriend even before they were separated.''

"Did she talk much about her husband? She was rooming here, rather than living at home with him, but did that add to their problems?''

Jonquil made a face, turning her even features into a waspish glare. ''I'm sure that Walter wasn't too happy about that, his 'property' taking off. You know, he tried to blame me for her decision to move out. I had nothing to do with it, though. When Erica wanted to leave Walter— and she'd decided to do that before she even knew me— she asked my brother if he knew of anyone with a room to rent. Of course he did, I'd been looking for a roommate for a few months. Anyway, when she told Walter he was history he blew up, tried to threaten her, smacked her around some. It scared the hell out of her.'' She shook her head sadly, remembering her friend's marital problems. ''He was such a control freak, I don't know why she ever married him. . . .''

''He threatened her, huh?'' Taylor narrowed her gaze, recognizing how that fit perfectly into the puzzle. Surely the note was just another manifestation of his authoritative nature. She'd have to get into Erica's room, see if she could track down some of his writing to verify that the note was from him. ''So, Jonquil—''

''Johnny, call me Johnny. Jonquil sounds so formal, and I'd say we're way past that.''

''Okay, Johnny, do you know what he did for a living?'' She was hoping to hear that he did something technical, something that could give him the background to sabotage a King Air. ''He didn't work in aviation, too, did he?''

''Nah, Mr. Control Freak was a friggin' car salesman. Not used cars—boy, wouldn't that fit a stereotype if he did?—but new cars. Erica said he sold Geos, that's how she got hers.'' Johnny peered out the window next to the dinner table and stared at the car in the driveway. ''Come to think of it, isn't that her car? I noticed it earlier, but it never clicked until just now. You borrowing it or something?''

''Yeah, I am. I had a little trouble with my car this morning, so I went to the LifeLine office to get hers.'' She scowled in remembrance of the morning's wreck—it made her mad that anyone could have targeted *her* for a hit.

A millisecond later another thought took her over: Walter Wolverton sold Geos?

Another car made by that manufacturer was the Tracker, a sport utility vehicle exactly like the Suzuki Sidekick. They didn't just look the same, they were the *identical* car, every sprocket and pin. No wonder her car got sabotaged; Walter Wolverton probably knew enough about Geo Trackers and Suzuki Sidekicks to tamper with them blindfolded!

But would that kind of knowledge enable him to rig the King Air to crash? she asked herself.

Sure it would, she deduced. Certainly he could read a maintenance manual with a practiced eye, and even if *he* couldn't, he would have access to mechanics who could.

But what about the threatening note? she wondered. What did that mean? She'd have to find something else to shed some light on that—maybe another clue could do it. She cleared her throat, and said, ''I met Erica's parents in Anchorage the other day, and she told me about her brother, Michael, but I don't know anything about her friends. Who'd she hang around with?''

Johnny laughed, a light, musical note. ''Pilots, pilots, pilots. She was so taken by aviation she wouldn't talk to anyone that didn't know it. The only reason she roomed here with a nonpilot is because my brother flew with her, and a bit of his aviation knowledge rubbed off on me.''

Ahhh. That was interesting—her friends were all pilots, and all of them would have known enough about mechanical things to sabotage an airplane or a car easily. Did she have something on one of them, something damaging enough to trigger murder?

Taylor pushed her chair away from the table and stood. ''Johnny, you said she hadn't moved everything to Anchorage. Can I look at what's left in her room? Her family hasn't cleared the stuff out, have they?''

"Nah, they haven't. I think it was about all they could handle for some time, just arranging for her memorial service. They didn't even take her computer, and I know there was a lot of stuff on her hard drive that they would've wanted to look at. She was trying to write a book, you know? In her spare time."

That surprised Taylor—the younger woman hadn't mentioned that to her, but they hadn't really known each other long enough to get into details like that.

Johnny stripped her sweatpants off and sat there in her white cotton underwear. The well-tuned look of her legs indicated that her afternoon run was not a singular event—the delineation of her quadriceps stood out from her thighs like bas-relief. "Anyway"—she glanced at her watch—"I need to get into the shower before I leave for work. You're welcome to poke around if you want. Her room is at the end, there." She gestured to the right of the kitchen, where a short hallway stretched down to a closed door. Carrying her sweatpants in one hand, she padded off in the opposite direction. "Holler at me if I'm still in the shower when you leave, okay?" she yelled over her shoulder.

Opening the door to Erica's room, Taylor peered around the corner before she stepped inside. The quarters were nearly bare—no sheets on the bed, no posters on the wall, no clothes in the small closet opposite the door. In one small alcove sat a few boxes holding paperback books—a quick peek showed the younger woman enjoyed reading mysteries.

A computer, a Macintosh Classic II, sat on a rolltop desk near a window looking into the garden, and Taylor walked over to it, curious about its contents. Reaching behind the compact machine, she flipped a switch and started it up—after a few hums and buzzes, the screen brightened. When she brought up the hard disk window, she saw the icon for a Microsoft Word program similar to the one LifeLine employed for word processing. Filling one corner of the monitor's window were several titled folders.

Betrayal 1–10 was the designation on one label, *Betrayal 11–20* the caption on the another. There it was, Erica's novel. Using the mouse, she looked into *Betrayal*, Chapter 1, and smiled as she scrolled through the prose. As she would have guessed, *Betrayal* was a mystery set in the world of aviation, complete with phrases and actions she recognized from her own experiences as a pilot.

"Well, they say, 'Write what you know,' " she muttered to the empty room. Grinning, she remembered a good friend from high school chanting that truism when she had decided to become a writer.

"Write what you know? Write what you know?" the friend had complained. "But I don't know anything yet. I'm just a junior in high school, for crying out loud!"

It looked like Taylor's coworker had been writing a fictionalized account of events from her own life as a copilot. Vaguely disguised but easy enough to spot if you knew Alaskan aviation.

As Taylor jumped from Chapter 1 to Chapter 2, the action took on a darker tone—the protagonist (Erica renamed as Annalee) had stumbled over some criminal activity she wanted to stop. She hadn't been able to finger the bad guy yet, and even though a threatening note had told her to back off, she was working hard toward finding a suspect.

But before any specifics were given about the illegal game afoot, the writing ended. The next chapters consisted of nothing but short synopses—only the first two chapters were finished. Taylor had to dissect the outlines to paste the story's plot together—the tale dealt with a pilot trafficking in drugs, flying them to remote Native villages around the state. Annalee discovers the illicit scheme and the man behind it, and he attempts to buy her silence by cutting her in on the profits. However, she refuses to accept his bribe, and declares her intent to go to the police. A wild climax ensues, when the villain attacks her, but she escapes and races him back to town to report him to the authorities.

By the time Taylor finished with the synopses, sweat was

trickling down her temples. How much of the story did Erica make up? Had she written from her own experience? Some of the plotline, like the offer to cut Annalee in on the profits, sounded too much like the note stuffed in the young copilot's jacket to be nothing but coincidence.

And Taylor didn't believe in coincidence.

But who were the fictional characters in real life? Was the portrayal of the criminal as a pilot modeled on someone Erica knew, maybe one of her many pilot friends?

Could Walter Wolverton be the villain, and was he the one that wrote the threatening note? Johnny Norback had already indicated he had a track record for intimidating his wife.

She glanced around the room, looking for some papers containing handwriting that matched the ominous warning, but nothing looked helpful. Erica must have moved most of her stuff to her new apartment.

The sound of the bathroom door swinging open interrupted her thought process, and Johnny poked her head out to ask if Taylor was still there.

"Yeah, Johnny, I'm still here," she called back. "But I'm packing up right now. Don't bother coming out to see me to the door. I can find my way. Thanks for letting me talk to you about Erica; you've been a great help."

More than Johnny would ever know.

EIGHTEEN

By the time Taylor maneuvered Erica's Geo Metro up the driveway to her cabin, she was mentally exhausted. Good thing it was only fall and there wasn't any snow on the ground—the small car wouldn't have been able to plow up the long path from the street to her yard. If she'd had to deal with digging it out of a snow berm, after her stressful day, it would have done her in.

As it was, she had to deal with other things that afternoon—her Suzuki still sat nose-deep in someone's front yard, and she needed to get it towed back home. Undoubtedly the people that lived there were wondering how to get rid of it, too.

She hoped they hadn't called the cops to report an abandoned vehicle on their property—perhaps fines and violations followed a citizen complaint, and she didn't need a big legal bill right then. Maybe the police wouldn't issue a citation because of the circumstances behind the accident, even though she had stupidly failed to call it in.

Anyway, finding a tow truck was the next item on her agenda—if she was lucky, the wrecker yards would still be open. She glanced at her watch and saw it was only five-thirty—maybe the tow trucks didn't charge for a late-hour call-out until after six o'clock.

Leaning against the compact's headrest, she inhaled deeply and exhaled slowly. She knew reclaiming her own car was a priority, but she felt so tired—odd, how emotional stress knocked the get-up-and-go out of you.

The deeper she got into the mystery surrounding the King Air wreck, the more she marveled at Homo sapiens' ability to plunge to immoral depths. How could anybody plot to kill another human, especially to protect their own involvement in criminal activities?

She snorted, then hauled herself out of the Geo and tromped across her front yard. Upon hanging her flight jacket on the coatrack inside the door, she headed to her answering machine and trained her tired eyes on it.

The blinking red light on the machine's base signaled the presence of two messages, so she wearily punched the playback button to retrieve them. Nate Mueller's voice blasted into the room when the first message began, and she lowered the machine's volume to stifle it. Why had she turned it up so loud? She wasn't deaf yet—give her a few more years.

Shrugging, she concentrated on what Nate was saying. "... me a call when you get home. You're going to have to fill in tonight for somebody else on the schedule. I'll give you the details when I talk to you." *Click!*

Oh, damn. The last thing she wanted to do that night was be on call for a medevac—what the hell happened to her week off?

The next message made things even worse—it was from Steve. "Taylor, it's me. We're in Corpus Christi, the patient has had a minor relapse, and the hospital doesn't want to let him go until he's stabilized. I don't know how long we'll be stuck here, but I wouldn't hold my breath if I were you. I'll call again when I get a better idea how things are going. Take care."

Rats—her plan for the night had included seeing him

later on. He would have been home by midnight, if things had gone as they should have, and by the time he arrived at her house she might have had an answer to the afternoon's questions. He'd be pissed when he heard how she had spent her time, but when he heard her sensible plan to deal with the matter he'd have to agree with her.

Only one problem, though—she didn't *have* a sensible plan yet.

Sighing, she picked up her cordless phone and headed for the living room. Once ensconced on the love seat, she tapped out Nate's number. Her head lolled back onto the sofa's arm as she counted rings, and three chirps later, he was on the line.

"Why are you doing this to me, wrecking my week off?" She knew that wasn't a very tactful way to deal with the bad news, but she felt abused. The call from Steve had left her on edge, and it showed. "Have I run out of good karma this year or what?"

"Oh, de-tune, Taylor," he teased. "Have you got a hot date for tonight or something? You must be getting a little on the side with Steve gone to Texas."

"Yeah, right. I just wanted to get some rest tonight, make some popcorn, do some reading." And do some more thinking about Erica's enigmatic writing. "Anyway, what's up?"

"Terry Pitts called me a few hours ago, seems he picked up a whale of a cold in Seattle. He's popping some pills for it—Actifed, or something—and he can't fly when he's taking those, because they make you drowsy. So if he doesn't want his head to explode he can't be on the schedule tonight or the next few days. You're the only King Air captain I have left that's not assigned to fly one of the ships, so you're next up for calls."

"Me? Why me? You've got other captains to choose from—"

Then she remembered he *didn't* have any more King Air captains to turn to—the other captain she'd automatically thought of was lying in a body bag in the medical examiner's refrigerated vault. "Oh, yeah, I forgot . . . Sorry."

"Yeah." His heavy sigh echoed across the phone line. "But who knows? You might not get a call tonight, so you won't have to leave your popcorn behind. Anyway, go ahead and turn your beeper on right now, and keep your fingers crossed."

Once they ended their conversation, she dropped the cordless on the sofa and reached for the phone book. She had to find a towing company that would drag the Suzuki home—she'd decide where to take it for its repairs later.

Halfway through *The Tonight Show,* Taylor began to relax, realizing she wouldn't have to fly that night. If no calls came in by twelve or one o'clock—and it was eleven-thirty by then—she would feel comfortable about going to bed. Usually, the pilots wouldn't get dispatched if it hadn't happened by midnight. That was a relief, since commanding a high-performance aircraft that evening might not be a wise move for her. The analysis of Erica's enigmatic writing still begged for attention, and she couldn't concentrate on anything else.

Jay Leno and his guest, funnyman Jim Carrey, traded jokes with each other as she stared at the TV screen with unfocused eyes. Even when the younger comedian performed one of his strings of hilarious facial contortions, she didn't twitch a muscle. Her hands were wrapped around a throw pillow like it was a life preserver and she was a passenger on the Titanic.

Who was the fictitious bad guy in Erica's book summary? She suspected it was Walter Wolverton—after all, he had threatened his wife in the past, and he had access to people who could have performed both acts of sabotage. Maybe the other woman had disguised her husband's physical characteristics in her writing to protect herself from a charge of libel—certainly, she'd read about those suits, and the need to guard against them.

Even more likely, Erica had hidden his true identity because their former relationship was an embarrassment. She didn't want the story's villain to look anything like her *husband.*

While Taylor brooded over her discovery at Johnny's house, her pager chirped and interrupted her thoughts. Her head jerked up from her chest, and a quick jolt of adrenaline stabbed her—every time she got beeped, she felt herself tense. It was time to go into overdrive, time to work— somebody was in trouble somewhere, and she was responsible for getting him or her back to safety.

She grabbed the small black box from the end table and identified the phone number displayed as the hospital's. A second later, the cordless was in her hands.

"Hey, there," she greeted the dispatcher. "This is Taylor, whatcha got for me?"

"Hi, Taylor, this is Suzanne. I got a call from Kodiak. Guy had a heart attack, needs to get into town to see a cardiologist. His condition is unstable—he's still fighting arrhythmia—so you guys need to hurry."

"We always do, Suzanne. Who's going with me?"

"Let's see." Paper crinkled as she looked at her clipboard. "Melissa Gwaltney and Kay Mahowald. They'll be on their way to the airport momentarily."

"Okay. I'll check weather and hightail it outta here. Later, Suzanne."

"See ya. Have a good trip."

Taylor hoped she would—an anxiety headache, spawned by her frenetic puzzling over Erica's writings, threatened to blossom into a full-blown skull knocker. She rarely had headaches, but the fact that one was rearing its ugly head at that moment didn't surprise her.

After tapping out the phone number for Flight Service, she reached over her shoulder for her notepad to copy the weather data.

•   •   •

Squealing into the LifeLine parking lot, Taylor thanked her lucky stars for the absence of patrol cars on her trip to the hangar. She was so used to her own car's stiff clutch and accelerator that the softer gas pedal on the aqua compact made for an interesting ride to the airport. On numerous occasions, she had to slow down to meet the speed limit, and she didn't know if rushing off for a medevac flight would warrant leniency from a police officer.

The lot was empty except for Cameron McNiven's Toyota pickup, and an unknown vehicle she assumed belonged to one of the nurses. After letting herself into the office, she headed for the lights shining from the locker room, and greeted her copilot. "Evening, Cam. I thought you'd be here."

"Hey, Taylor." He glanced up with a smile on his face and finished fastening the zipper of his coveralls. As per usual, his coveralls looked freshly ironed, the creases as tight as an Air Force uniform. His leather flight case sat on the wooden bench at his side; his jacket was slung over the door to his locker.

"I figured Nate'd call you up to play stand-in for Terry," he said.

"Well, you were right. However, I'm not sure if I'm up to pulling your butt out of the fire tonight, so you'd better be on your best behavior."

"Aww, you're not still bent out of shape because of that little run-in from the other day, are you?" He shrugged into his flight jacket and grabbed his flight case.

"Little run-in? I wouldn't call taxiing out in front of a Boeing 727 *little*! You gotta promise me you won't do that tonight." Even though she sounded angry, she was just teasing—she wasn't going to let him live that faux pas down.

"Oh, come on, Taylor. You know there's no way I could've hit that Boeing; they're way too big," he joked. He reached over to plant a quick peck on her cheek like an apology.

Her eyes widened—he'd never done anything like *that* before.

He stepped back from her, as though checking on her reaction to the kiss. "Anyway," he continued in a placating tone, "I'm not going to do anything to endanger my favorite captain."

"Oh, give me a break," she blustered. "Go do your preflight." He grinned and walked over to the door to the hangar, pushing through it.

What was that kiss for? she wondered once he left. Was he coming on to her? Or was it nothing but a friendly gesture of affection? If the kiss indicated some interest on his part, that was a fact to be put on the back burner, savored a bit. Maybe she'd think about that on the way to Kodiak, see if he continued to act touchy-feely like that with her as they flew.

Ironic. It flattered her to be seen as a woman when: number one, the person doing the seeing is really attractive; number two, you're desperate for distraction; and number three, your boyfriend's stuck in Texas indefinitely.

Stepping into her coveralls, she hid the smirk on her face.

NINETEEN

Halfway home from Kodiak—approximately one hundred miles from Anchorage—Taylor looked over her shoulder into the cabin. "Everything okay back there?" she asked.

One of the flight nurses answered, her eyes trained on the portable EKG monitor propped near their patient. "I'm not sure. These arrhythmias are getting worse." Melissa Gwaltney pushed her horn-rim glasses further back up the bridge of her nose and peered more intently at the machine's screen. She wore the nurse's version of the Nomex flight suit the pilots had on, with the addition of a stethoscope draped around her neck and hemostats poking out of her cargo pockets. Like all of the flight nurses, she was slim—lifting patients in and out of aircraft kept one in fighting trim.

Melissa turned to her partner, Kay Mahowald. "All right, we'd better start a lidocaine drip for the PCVs." The other nurse grabbed a vial of a clear liquid and began administering it to the patient through the IV tube inserted in his fleshy arm.

The man lying on the bench looked like a prime subject

for a heart attack. If he hadn't suffered the one that put him on the medevac flight to Anchorage that night, one certainly would have been in the near future. He looked like a Sumo wrestler—excess flesh hung from his arms, and he had breasts that would have made a stripper proud. Tobacco stains darkened his gritted teeth, and his wheezing filled the cabin of the droning aircraft.

In contrast, the fit Kay Mahowald was only a quarter of his weight, but her size belied her toughness. With her own eyes Taylor had seen her heft one end of a stretcher laden down by a man nearly as big as the one she presently worked on. Her squeaky voice and blond Dorothy Hamill haircut didn't help in making her look formidable, but she was a nurse the aircraft's captain would have picked for her flight team any day of the year.

Only a matter of minutes after the nurse had started the lidocaine drip, her coworker raised her voice in apprehension. "He's in V-tach, Kay. Get the defibrillator ready."

Taylor swung around in her seat, alerted by the tone of Melissa's voice that they had trouble. She also knew what V-tach meant—ventricular tachycardia indicated a heart in severe distress.

"We gotta defib this guy, Taylor," Melissa called out. "I wanted to let you know what was going on, okay?"

Ten seconds later, the bespectacled nurse had the defibrillator paddles poised above the patient's chest. "Clear!" she yelled to warn her partner, and planted them firmly in place. The man's torso convulsed as the electricity surged through his body, but the line on the EKG still showed irregular sine waves that indicated the heart hadn't come out of V-tach yet.

"He's not responding, Kay, go with the epinephrine. I'm gonna bag him and start CPR." As Taylor watched anxiously—she hated to witness intubation—Melissa raised the man's chin and fed a tube down his trachea, the bag attached to the rubber line hand-delivering oxygen to the lungs like a bellows. Once it was inserted in the man's windpipe, she pushed the bag at her coworker, who had finished injecting the medicine into the IV line.

With her hands free, Melissa leaned over to begin CPR. Crossing her hands over the man's sternum, she used her weight to compress his chest as Kay squeezed the oxygen bag. However, the EKG only showed a wavy line without the peaks that would indicate a properly beating heart.

The flight nurse pushed her glasses up again, her light brown hair beginning to darken with sweat. The armpits of her coveralls were already damp. "He's still not responding to the epinephrine, try more lidocaine. I'm gonna defibrillate him again."

Grabbing the paddles, Melissa raised them above the patient's chest. "Clear!" she ordered as she pushed them down. The electricity contorted the patient again, but the EKG line didn't break into a different rhythm.

Taylor saw that the action in the cabin was building—Melissa had begun the CPR once more, stopping every five compressions to squeeze the oxygen bag Kay had abandoned to inject more lidocaine. "Take over," she directed her copilot when she realized how busy the nurses were getting. "I'm going back to help." His eyes widened nervously as she climbed out of her seat and headed into the cabin.

"What can I do?" she asked Melissa as she stood over the patient's head.

"Here, take this." The nurse handed Taylor the oxygen bag, relief displayed in her eyes when help came. "Squeeze it every five seconds, keep it regular, while I continue the CPR." She resumed her earlier actions, pumping down on the man's chest, monitoring the EKG.

"Damn, he's still not responding!" she cursed. "I'm going to defibrillate him again. Kay, get some bretylium ready." She reached for the paddles, shouting "Clear!" before applying them. The man spasmed a third time, but the screen still showed nothing.

Kay shot the bretylium into the IV tube, staring agape at

the EKG. The line on the monitor was nearly flat, nothing but tiny rough squiggles breaking up from the horizontal. "He's in V-fib, Melissa!" she cried.

Taylor, her eyes as big as saucers, glanced at one nurse, then the other. She knew what V-fib meant, too—ventricular fibrillation represented the last gasps of a dying heart. "What are you going to do now? He's not coming out of it."

"Yeah, I know. . . . But I still gotta . . . keep up the CPR," Melissa grunted as she pushed down on the patient's chest. "We gotta . . . keep going, we can't . . . stop the CPR . . . and declare him dead. . . . Only a doctor . . . can do that." She swiped at her forehead a second time— her bangs were dripping by then. "Go ahead and . . . go back up front. . . . Call base and tell them . . . we've got a Code ninety-nine. . . . Kay and I can handle . . . the CPR . . . by ourselves. . . . There's nothing else . . . to do back here."

Taylor stared at the obese form lying in front of her. She knew the nurses would continue to give him CPR, to try to bring him back to life, but it was obvious to her that he was gone. She felt like *she'd* failed somehow, though she had nothing to do with his death. The nurses hadn't caused his demise, either—they had done everything they could, as well as they could, but the man was not destined to recover from his heart attack.

Shaken, she backed up to the cockpit, her eyes never leaving the inert form on the stretcher. She nearly tripped over the flight cases in the aisle between the pilot's seats, but caught herself before she fell. Awkwardly, she settled into her seat, still focused on the man in the cabin.

Melissa and Kay continued to perform CPR on their patient, but nothing registered on the EKG. He was gone.

Taylor lowered herself onto the wooden bench in the locker room and stared at her feet. The sounds of a nurse yelling "Clear!" and the thud of the patient convulsing under the defibrillator rang in her head—the image of an ambulance, rushing off to the hospital with its lights flashing, still strobed across her mind. She couldn't push the pictures away. The scene she had witnessed had devastated her.

"You've never had a patient die on a flight before, have you?" Cameron asked quietly. He sat down next to her and put his arm around her shoulders. "I can still remember the first one they lost on a plane I was flying. It hurt."

"Yeah, it does. I can't believe I've flown medevacs this long without having a death on my plane." She looked up and met his eyes, his presence comforting her. "I feel like it was my fault, like I didn't fly fast enough or something. Did you feel that way when a patient died on your plane?"

"Sure, it's human nature." He edged over closer to her, the fabric of their coveralls swishing when their thighs touched. "It's weird how your head can lie to you when you're upset like that. There wasn't any way I could've saved the patient's life, but I was convinced I had done something wrong. It was my third flight in the King Air, and I was sure that if I'd had more experience in the aircraft, the guy wouldn't have died. The fact that the patient had five bullet holes in his chest didn't sway my opinion a bit."

She snorted. "I wonder if it ever gets any easier—" She shook her head, exhaustion retarding the movement. It had been a rotten day, a long day. A single tear trickled down her cheek, and she brushed it away immediately. She hated crying, even if she *was* tired and upset.

He reached over to touch the path the tear had taken. "Yeah, it does get easier, Taylor. This is the worst it'll be." He cupped her chin in his hand and tipped her lips up to meet his. Before it even registered in her fatigued mind, their lips touched and they kissed, gently at first, then more passionately.

Halfway through the kiss, her eyes blinked open and she pulled her head back. "No, I can't do this, Cam." She wasn't going to betray Steve. Even though they weren't married, or even engaged, there was an implicit agreement between them—they dated each other exclusively. Kissed each other exclusively. Made love to each other exclusively.

He may have been in Texas, but out of sight was *not* out of mind—she wasn't going to step out on him. They may have their disagreements, like how to handle the King Air crash investigation, but she wouldn't absolve her lack of control by saying she was just upset and vulnerable. Having a traumatic day didn't give her carte blanche to ignore her lover's feelings.

Cameron seemed to ignore her withdrawal from his kiss, and moved his face back within two inches of hers. "Hey, you're just upset," he said smoothly. "It's not easy, having a guy die on your plane. I can make you feel better, though. Let me do that for you." His left hand caressed the upper part of her thigh, and he gently parted her lips with his own.

She pulled her head back again and scooted away from him on the bench. "No, Cam," she muttered. "I don't think this is a good idea. Let's just go home. You to your house, me to mine." She stood and began to pull her coveralls off her street clothes.

TWENTY

Raindrops pinged off the bubble window in Taylor's sleeping loft, driven by a brisk, cold northerly wind. She drew the comforter off her face and peered up at the Plexiglas window, seeing nothing but dark, gray clouds hovering slightly above the cabin.

"Oh, shit," she muttered to the empty room. "This'll be fun to fly in." Dragging the down-filled piece back over her head, she hid herself from the nasty weather outside. It didn't look fit for man or beast.

Or medevac pilot.

Five seconds later, she sighted on the hands of her watch which glowed in the under-the-covers dimness: 11:20 a.m.

Her eyes spread wide and she jerked the comforter off her face again. Shit, it was almost noon! She couldn't believe she'd slept that long—even though she hadn't gotten to bed until four o'clock that morning, she normally would have been up by seven. Her body seemed programmed for that—even though she woke tired, she still woke.

Shaking the fog from her head, she rolled over and decided that maybe this one time she could pardon herself for her sloth. If it wasn't for those nightmares, she thought, she might have gotten more rest once she'd lain down, and risen at a decent hour. Fleeting images of danger had bounced around her brain once she'd fallen asleep, making those nocturnal hours useless as refreshers, and she hadn't gotten anything out of them.

Thankfully, there was only one image she could recall from the nightmares, but that singular mental snapshot was enough to get her heart chattering again. In the vision, she had found herself watching helplessly from a rocky beach as Erica Wolverton thrashed and gasped in the deep water offshore. The younger woman's head would bob up, sink under the surface, then break through again as her arms flogged the water wildly. She was obviously drowning.

Even though she had scuba gear on, for some reason the tanks on her back were not supplying her with oxygen, and she wasn't able to keep her head out of the water. It appeared that someone or something was dragging her below the whitecapped darkness.

The screams of the frantic woman still echoed in Taylor's head, and in an attempt to silence them she buried herself back under the covers. As she lay there, she felt odd. There had been something important about the troubling nightmare, she was sure of it, but in the light of the gray day it would not reveal itself again. It just dangled there on the edge of her consciousness, teasing her with its significance, maddeningly elusive.

She pulled the comforter down and sat up in bed. When she stripped it off her nearly naked body, the vivid chrome yellow cotton of her underwear caught her eye. Smiling, she appreciated the bright contrast they made to the gloomy haze outside—she knew there was a reason why she'd bought such a bold color. And it wasn't just because they'd make her easier to find in the dark, like Steve had quipped.

With her legs dangling over the side of the mattress, she started making plans for the rest of the day, whatever was left of it. Maybe she'd stop by the gym, work out a bit. She'd been so preoccupied with the recent tragedy that her normal exercise routine had been shot down in flames. She'd better get back into the routine, before her muscles atrophied and her flight suit would not fit.

Anyway, until Steve got back—and who knew when that would be—she didn't want to do any more amateur sleuthing. She needed to run her findings past him, regardless of how he'd react to it—he had a logical mind, and she could use a second perspective on Erica's fictionalized autobiography. He would see it differently, no doubt, but maybe his view would spark some kind of understanding for her. Something she could show to the NTSB.

While she waited for him to return, she had another night of being on call to look forward to. From the picture of the wet, blustery day outside, she hoped she didn't have to fly anywhere that night—the combination of rain-slicked runways, tough crosswinds, and deepening darkness was not one she cared for.

Reaching for a pair of scuffs that peeked out from under the bed, she struggled to stick a foot into one. Her big toe got caught on the slipper's opening, so she swore at it and pulled it off to try again. As she struggled with it, the phone bleated, and she jumped, startled by the unanticipated noise.

The other phone downstairs chimed in, as well, and she had the racket of two phones—both set on HI—dueling it out in the confines of the small cabin. She snatched up the nearest one, which silenced both, and sighed in relief.

Assuming it was Steve checking in, she dropped the timbre of her voice, making it sultry. "Speak to me," she said throatily, like a phone sex operator. She thought if she really worked at it she could get him all hot and bothered long-distance.

That could be fun.

Even though she'd rejected Cameron McNiven's advances the previous evening, it wasn't as though it hadn't affected her. She was a healthy woman, with healthy hormones, and his touch—unwanted or not—had stirred them. Her beau's return could not come sooner.

"Good morning, Taylor. You sound like you're in a good mood this morning."

The voice on the line startled her—it wasn't Steve, it was Cameron, and she verbally backtracked hastily. "Hey, I thought you were someone else."

"So you didn't answer the phone that way for my benefit? Damn. I was hoping the good mood meant you had reconsidered what happened at the hangar. Or rather, what *didn't* happen at the hangar."

"Well, things haven't changed, Cam. It's not that you're not attractive, but—" She curled her feet under her butt and stared out the window. Gold leaves were dropping off the birch trees in her backyard, propelled by the gusty wind. "Anyway, let's just forget it."

"Hmmm. Well, you can't blame a guy for trying. I thought I'd just grab the opportunity to comfort you when I saw how upset you were. And that's all it was, you know, some comforting. . . ."

"You've got an odd idea of what comfort entails." She didn't believe his explanation—maybe she was just flattering herself, but a serious kiss usually meant more.

"Oh, cut me some slack here, lady. It really *was* just an attempt to get you feeling better. I wanted to because we're friends, and friends do that for each other. And if anything else had happened as a result, well, I wouldn't have said no. You're a good-looking woman, and sometimes comfort has more than one face." He cleared his throat.

She hoped he was uncomfortable with trying to explain why he put the moves on her.

He spoke up again. "Well, maybe you're right. Let's just forget any of this happened, okay? Let's call it a difference of opinion, a little misunderstanding. We can stay friends, can't we?"

She sighed. "Okay, we can try." She wasn't sure that was the best track to follow, but it probably was the most diplomatic. After all, they still had to work together, and for all she knew, they might have to fly together that night.

"Hey, great," he said happily. "I'm glad you agree. Why don't we get some lunch together, get back to being friends again? How do you feel about some Thai food. I know you like that."

"All right, why don't we meet at the Thai restaurant on Northern Lights near Minnesota? That's kind of close to the hangar, and I want to stop there after lunch."

"It's a deal. I'll see you in a half hour."

"Let's make it an hour. I gotta take a shower. Wash the medevac sweat off me."

After cradling the phone, she stepped out of her underwear and into the second scuff. Climbing down the loft's ladder, dragging a terry-cloth robe behind her, she headed for her bathroom.

TWENTY-ONE

The short, fifty-foot dash from the Geo to the door of the Thai restaurant left Taylor's face peppered with raindrops. It wasn't that a downpour had caught her—it rarely rained hard in arid Southcentral Alaska—but the drops were not falling vertically, but horizontally. The cold north wind hadn't abated, either, its velocity increasing from twenty knots to about thirty. Tiny waves striated the deepening puddles on the asphalt square in front of the restaurant—little wind vortices agitated the piles of sodden leaves scattered in a nearby vacant lot.

The restaurant's front door bumped closed behind her after she burst through it, shaking the water off her face and the shoulders of her flight jacket. She hated getting the leather wet, but hadn't thought of wearing a different coat until after she'd left the cabin.

Once she was out of the storm, she sputtered, "Whew!" and stomped her muddy boots on a sisal mat by the door. Her hair looked like it had been run through a blender set on frappé, and the chill of the wind had pinked her cheeks.

Folding back her jacket's mouton collar, she scanned the small room for Cameron. She was a little late—the shower had felt really good that morning for some reason—and she hoped he hadn't been waiting too long.

He was perched on a chair at a corner table near a window, eyeing the weather outside, unaware of her entrance. A yellow slicker was draped over the seat next to him— he'd had the sense to dress for the rain, unlike her.

She trotted over, apologizing. "Sorry I'm late. I got so waterlogged in the shower that my pants wouldn't fit until I'd wrung my legs out. You weren't getting bored waiting for me, were you?"

His gaze swung from the window toward her. "Hey, no problem." He was looking typically well groomed that afternoon—the medevac flight's late arrival into Anchorage didn't appear to have ruffled his feathers. The collar of his raspberry polo shirt was jauntily turned up from the crew neck of his navy-blue cotton sweater, and every strand of his hair was in place—a thirty-knot wind didn't appear to be blowing on the planet *he* lived on.

Settling into her seat, she admired his ability to retain his coif in the midst of a storm. "How do you do that, Cam?" she asked him, pointing at his hair.

"How do I do what?" he replied, acting like he didn't know what she was talking about.

"Oh, never mind." Obviously, he didn't want to discuss his preening techniques, so she just gestured at the nasty picture developing outside. "Nice day, huh? I hope we don't get a call-out tonight. It wouldn't be much fun."

His gaze returning to the window, he commented, "Yeah, you're right about that. If it's kinda bumpy because of the wind, the flight nurses or the patient might get airsick. It amazes me that that doesn't happen more often. I've only seen it once, and it was really turbulent then. I was turning a bit green myself that time." He grinned in retrospect.

"Well, it's making me airsick just thinking about it. Let's not try to gross each other out by telling horror stories, okay? At least not until after lunch." She reached for the menu resting near her silverware and began to study it. She didn't really need to—she got the same thing nearly every time she ate Thai food—but she thought that looking at her menu would preempt any more discussion of violent stomach distress.

When the waitress appeared to take their orders, Taylor decided upon her usual, Pad Thai Vegetable, and he pointed at number 101 on the menu, Yum Talay, spinach and tofu doused with peanut sauce. Both of them got heaping helpings of rice to go with the food.

While waiting for their meals, they chitchatted of this and that. How long did Terry Pitts think he'd be laid up? How did Taylor like the new King Air, now that she'd had a chance to fly it? Was Cam ready for winter yet, and was he going to do any downhill skiing this year?

Neither of them mentioned the disturbing scene at the hangar. Even though it had happened less than twelve hours ago, no discussion ensued. It had been swept under the rug, as though it hadn't occurred.

She felt better about the whole thing, actually—her co-worker was back to his old style, dryly witty and self-deprecating, eager to make her laugh at his own expense. Maybe his kiss really had been nothing but an attempt to make her feel better, not an attempt to get in her pants. His idea of how to console her had been very different from her own, but maybe that was okay. The world would be a boring place if everyone reacted the same way to everything.

When their food arrived, they tore into it. He appeared to be as hungry as she was, and few words passed between them other than, "Can I have some water?" and "Hand me another napkin, would you?" Fifteen minutes passed before their food-shoveling marathon showed any signs of ending.

Finally, Taylor laid her fork down. Normally, she used chopsticks to eat Thai food, but she couldn't stuff the food into her mouth fast enough with them so she turned to conventional utensils. "Wow, that was good," she pronounced. "Usually I can't eat my entire meal, and I have to take half of it home in a doggie bag for dinner. That's one of the things I like about Thai food—it's cheap, and they give you a lot."

"Yeah, that *was* a lot. I ate enough in that one meal to give me Popeye's recommended daily allowance of spinach. Whew . . ." He rubbed his belly appreciatively.

Seeing that they were done, the waitress returned with the check. Cameron looked at the ticket briefly, then pulled out his MasterCard and offered it to her. She accepted it, but Taylor objected immediately.

"Hey, this is Dutch treat, put that away," she scolded. She reached for her own wallet and started rifling through it.

"Oh, come on, Taylor, let me put this on my card. I get Alaska Airlines sky miles for every dollar I charge on it. Since the LifeLine pilots don't get to fly non-rev, it sure helps."

She glanced up from her wallet, then shrugged. "Okay, go ahead and put it on your card. I do the same thing with mine, charge to get those air miles." She nodded her assent, so he shooed the waitress away. The diminutive ebony-haired woman disappeared in the direction of the cash register.

"These Alaska Airlines MasterCards are pretty cool," Taylor acknowledged. "I charge everything on mine—groceries, gas, my phone bill, even my visits to the dentist." She pulled her credit card out of her wallet and waved it around with a grin. "I even charged all of the lumber and supplies when I built my cabin. Boy, did that rack up the miles! I used some of them for quick jaunts down to Seattle earlier this summer, but I *still* have miles left over." She slid the card back in its slot in her wallet and laid the wallet on the table.

The *cachunk-cachunk* sound of the waitress running Cameron's MasterCard through the imprinter could be heard in the background, followed by the light shuffle of the woman's feet as she returned to where they sat. "Here you go, sir," the woman trilled, handing the card and the bill to him and offering a pen. "Come see us again." She smiled at him, then backed away from the table.

"Sure will," he replied, and bent down to add a tip to the total and sign the credit slip. When he had finished his signature, Taylor snatched it up. "Hey," he complained.

"I'll give it back, don't worry. I just gotta see what my share is, so I can give you the cash right here. That way, you get the miles for it but it's still Dutch treat." She peered at the onionskin paper of the slip and ran her finger down the numbers on the side. "Okay, half of sixteen is eight. I owe you that much."

Before she returned the slip, her glance landed on his signature. It was as clean and crisp as he was, organized, not frilly. She stared at his writing, the entire signature in capitals, and froze.

The blood drained from her face—the writing looked familiar.

In less than a second, a string of images flashed across her mind. The diver's weight belt wrapped around Jonquil Norback's waist. The photo of Cameron McNiven sleeping in his airplane after a scuba session, a rocky beach in the background. The cropped snapshot of Erica, wearing what Taylor finally realized was the bottom half of a diver's dry suit, sitting on the same beach.

Not only had he known the dead woman—even though he professed he only recognized her as the daughter of his mother's friend—he had known her well enough to take her diving with him and allow her to take photos of him. In addition, he was a pilot with his own plane, just like the younger woman had portrayed the criminal in her fictionalized autobiography.

Obviously, he was the one that had penned the threatening note on the back of the three-by-five photo. He had rigged the King Air to crash, taking Erica down with it.

With a brother who worked as a mechanic, and his own knowledge of aircraft, the sabotage had probably been child's play for him.

Taylor looked up from the credit slip, her face expressionless, deadpan. She didn't want him to see any emotion on her features that could alert him—if he knew she'd figured it out, it could mean trouble.

Grabbing his slicker from the other chair, he pulled it on and reached for the credit slip. He laid it on the table and nodded toward the restaurant's door with a smile. "You ready to go?" he asked, not appearing to notice anything untoward.

"Yeah," she answered, and stood up to turn away from the table. She retrieved her wallet and handed him eight dollars routinely.

"I need to go to the hangar," she added matter-of-factly, praying that no tremor could be detected in her speech— she wasn't a good actor. At the moment, she was terrified, and wished she could disguise it.

Halfway through the front door, thinking that she might have successfully escaped his notice, she heard a *click!* and felt something hard shoved up against her kidneys. A shot of adrenaline surged through her body; her spine stiffened. "Let's take my car," he said pleasantly, pushing her toward his Toyota.

She glanced over her shoulder, the horror plain in her features. "What are you—"

"Oh, come on, Taylor. You know what this is. I would've had to do this today anyway, but you fucked up my timetable." He shrugged and motioned for her to open the passenger's-side door of his truck. "I didn't think you'd figure it out. I suppose it's just as well, though, I would've felt terrible if I had to kill you and you didn't even know why. But this way, everything's on the table. So to speak." He jabbed her again in the lower back. "Get in, then slide over to the driver's side. You do know how to drive a stick shift, don't you?" He looked uncertain, then smiled in relief. "Oh, yes, of course you do. Your Suzuki's a stick."

She clambered into the Toyota and slid over as ordered. "But, Cam—" she tried to reason.

He appeared to ignore her attempt to speak to him, and followed her into the vehicle. "I never knew Suzukis were so fucking hard to work on. Nothing is where you can reach it. Good thing I've got a brother who's a mechanic. I wouldn't have been able to find those damn brake bleeders without his help. Anyway, go ahead and drive. We're heading for the Lake Hood strip; that's where my plane is."

Her eyes bulging out, she felt her knees become rubber. Oh, good Lord, she despaired, what was he thinking of? They were going flying, in this weather?

God.

If she didn't die from a bullet wound, fighting the wind and rain in a small plane certainly could result in the same thing.

TWENTY-TWO

W *hap . . . whap . . . whap . . . whap . . . whap . . .*
The wipers beat a steady rhythm on the Toyota's windshield, accompanying the rapid thump of Taylor's heart on her eardrums. She worked the clutch and brakes like an automaton, her legs feeling like putty. The food she'd gulped down during lunch threatened to come up—her stomach churned and gurgled in distress.

The tops of the birch trees bordering Northern Lights Boulevard bent in the wind whipping over them—dead leaves danced frantically across the road and plastered themselves against a nearby muddy slope. Even with the wipers set on HI, her vision of the road was blurred.

Light midday traffic filed by, the drivers oblivious to the drama playing out in the opposite lane. However, the peril she found herself in was much too obvious to *her*.

She could feel the cold steel of the gun barrel thrust against her ribs, and it served to focus her attention on an escape plan. She had to find a way to get away from Cameron, preferably before becoming airborne.

As she drove, she racked her brain to no avail. Within five to six minutes they would arrive at the Lake Hood airstrip, untie his plane, and depart the Anchorage Bowl in it. She had little time to devise a plan.

What if she just leaped from the vehicle upon slowing for the next stop sign? She could bolt for the nearest stand of trees, and the birches would hide her from the gunfire sure to follow her. Would that work?

She quickly decided no—the trees were too far from the street, he'd have plenty of time to shoot at her while she ran for cover. Plus, the only stop sign between them and the Lake Hood strip was at Lake Hood itself, and there were no trees there at all.

Shit.

Well, what if she swerved into the oncoming traffic? That could bring an immediate stop to the vehicle, as well as Cameron's plans, and probably bring the police, too.

But no, that wouldn't work either. When the wreck occurred, he'd know he was in trouble and had to get out of there. All he'd have to do then was shoot her, throw her out of the Toyota, and race off in it. Of course, he'd be leaving the scene of an accident, but who cares? That would be the least of his worries. Anyway, she couldn't bring herself to cause an accident—that might injure or kill an innocent person. Like her.

The truck was nearing the intersection of Northern Lights Boulevard and Airport Drive, only two minutes from their intended destination, when an idea flashed across her mind. Her mind grasped at it, digested it—yes, it might work, all she'd have to do is stay cool until the moment was right.

Could she do that? she wondered. Could she concentrate on waiting, not revealing her strategy, even while she was dragged closer and closer to disaster?

Cameron had a track record of indifference to the value of human life, that was obvious. Hadn't he plotted to rid himself of one person, killing four more in the process? He certainly hadn't anguished over the possibility of *her* death, either, when he rigged her Suzuki to kill or maim her. With all that in mind, could she stay calm when her instincts for survival begged her to fight back, save herself?

Well, she had no choice. She'd have to do it, regardless of the difficulty in stifling her impulse for self-preservation. Ordering herself to ease the stiffness in her spine, stay cool, she decided to get Cameron talking, find out what he had in mind for her. That could radically influence her plan to escape.

Filled by dread, not sure what she would hear, she turned to him. "How do you think you'll get away with this?" she asked. Gripping the steering wheel white-knuckled, her features pale, she felt the gusts rock the Toyota from side to side. "What are you going to do when you get called out on a medevac tonight and I never show up? Don't you think someone will be concerned about my whereabouts, ask you where I am?"

"No, I'm not worried about that," he replied, his tone of voice tempered and cool. He didn't appear to be the least bit excited by what he intended to do. "Why would I know where you went, anyway? I'd just say that we had lunch together this afternoon, and when we parted company you said you were going to the hangar. I wouldn't know you hadn't shown up." He chuckled, delighted by having the upper hand.

A bead of sweat trickled down her temple, and she felt like she was going to toss her lunch. She hoped Cameron didn't see her apprehension—the last thing she wanted was his realization of her terror.

"What about the other people who know what I've found?" she pointed out. "They know I was on to you, they'll finger you immediately as my murderer."

"No, no, Taylor. That's not going to work. I won't fall for the 'someone else knows' ploy. You had no idea I was behind anything until you saw something at lunch. It wasn't in your eyes, you didn't know shit until then—"

"That's where you're wrong, Cameron. You may think I didn't know anything until today, but I did. As soon as I looked at Erica's computer, I had it figured out. The story of your drug smuggling, and her refusal to help you with it, is all there in black-and-white. Add that to the threatening note you sent her, and it was easy to see her death in the King Air was not caused by pilot error.'' She snickered, trying to sound sure of herself even though she was terrified. ''Killing me won't save your ass, either. Someone else will see the same things I did, and pin Erica's murder on you. Even if they never connect you to *my* death, you'll be in deep shit for everything else. Five innocent people are dead because of you—you're going to fry for it, I guarantee.''

''Fry? Oh, come on, Taylor. Aren't you getting a little melodramatic?'' He laughed again, his cackling as painful as the sound of fingernails on a chalkboard. ''They're never going to catch me, and you know it. I'm not going to leave any tracks. I didn't leave any when I was running the dope to the villages, and I didn't leave any when I rigged the King Air.'' Another biting laugh erupted from him. ''As it turned out, killing Erica was really easy—I couldn't have planned it that well if I'd tried. Having Price on that flight turned out to be just what I needed to confuse everybody looking into the crash. As far as anyone is concerned, the findings of the NTSB are correct. The plane flew into Mt. Iliamna because Marshall Price had a heart attack and his *copilot* couldn't handle the aircraft on her own.''

He laughed, the barrel of the revolver ratcheting up and down her ribs as his gun arm shook. ''A heart attack, that's rich! He may have had symptoms of that IHSS stuff, but I can guarantee you that wasn't what killed him. Scott and I made sure of that; we weren't going to rely on chance. A little tweak to the oxygen system, and it was lights out.'' He seemed at ease with his plan, gleeful because he'd thought of all of the pitfalls in it. ''Anyway, you just happened to stumble over the right combination to solve the puzzle, and lightning isn't going to strike twice. 'Nuff said.'' He gestured with the gun, indicating that she should turn left at the next intersection.

Small aircraft on wheels clustered around the side of the road. One hundred yards ahead of the intersection more aircraft, these on floats, were moored on the shore of Lake Hood. The bright paint schemes of the seaplanes—yellow-and-black, red-and-white, blue-and-gold—contrasted sharply against the gray of the whitecapped water. Even though all the planes were secured to the ground or docks by nylon ropes, they jigged like marionettes when gusts hammered them.

"Yeah, I'm not going to leave any tracks, that's for sure," he mused, the tone of his voice shifting, as though he was talking to himself. "I've thought about it, a lot. That's why I'm not going to get rid of the body right here in town, leave bloodstains or fibers as evidence—I've seen enough cop shows on TV to know what they look for. And they won't find anything in my truck or my plane, either. No, I'm going to wait until I'm on the other side of the inlet to do the killing, bury the body somewhere in the woods. That's wilderness over there, thousands and thousands of acres of virgin forest. No one will find anything for years, if ever, and by that time there'll be nothing left to identify anyway." He grinned, his eyes unfocused, reciting his plan to ensure himself that he had taken every possible snag into account.

Then he snapped back to reality like someone flipped a switch, and waved the gun again. "My Cub is tied down at the south end of the strip; pull in there. Park right behind it."

When she slid out of the Toyota, Cameron using the gun's muzzle to goad her along, the vicious wind hit head-on and sucked the breath out of her. Her flight jacket flapped at her sides; her hair whipped around her face. The Super Cub strained against its restraints like an eager greyhound. Across the strip, a neon-orange traffic cone blew past and became wedged underneath a single-engine Citabria.

She flinched every time a fat raindrop stung her cheek,

each of her pilot's instincts warning her about the inclement weather—only an aviator with a death wish would venture into it. "Cam, you can't fly in this shit," she pleaded. "Can't you see that? If we go up, we could crash. And *you* could be killed, too, if that happens!"

He glared at her, his hair sticking out from the sides of his head like wings—his styling gel had finally lost its grip, and he looked wild, demonic, tufts of his dark brown hair being buffeted by the wind. "I have every confidence in you, Taylor. I know you can handle this weather. You're the one who's going to be flying, anyway."

"What? I can't fly your Cub. I don't have any tail-dragger time! I'll wreck it for sure!" She hoped that he loved his plane so much he wouldn't trust it to someone without knowledge of handling a tail-dragger, an aircraft with one of the wheels mounted in the rear of the fuselage. Tail-draggers were notoriously squirrelly in strong winds and required specialized training to make them perform properly.

Shaking his head, he appeared disappointed with her. "Nice try, but no cigar. I know you have tail-dragger time; you've talked about your dad teaching you to fly his Cessna one-eighty-five. If you can handle a one-eighty-five, you can handle a Super Cub. *I'm* certainly not going to fly. I'll be busy watching you." He motioned with his revolver. "Go get the Cub untied, we gotta get out of here."

With trembling hands, she unfastened both of the ropes tied to U-hooks on the wing struts. The whole time she told herself that things were going to be fine, just fine, once she'd enacted her plan for escape.

Well, not really fine, but at least she'd be free of Cameron's murderous intents.

TWENTY-THREE

Once Taylor had untethered the Piper Super Cub and wedged herself into the pilot's seat, she started the engine and taxied to the south end of the short gravel strip. The airplane rocked like a carnival ride as the gusts pummeled it—she had to use all of her pilot's skill to keep it upright and traveling a straight path. The stress of battling the wind, and the struggle to keep her wits about her, had her shaking, her breath coming in soundless gasps.

Out of the corner of her eye she could see trees, a quarter mile off to the east, bent over in the bluster of the north wind. Single raindrops trickled down the Plexiglas windshield of the airplane, forming rivulets as they combined with others in their mad dash groundward.

Cameron had taken his seat right behind her, the steel of the gun barrel pressed tightly against her nape. She never heard the click of his lap belt being fastened when he sat down—it appeared he expected some escape attempt from her, and wanted no restraint to his movement. Punctuating his wariness wordlessly, he prodded her with the muzzle of the gun.

The feel of cold steel lying aside her carotid artery had

a surreal quality to it—was this really happening to her, or was it a nightmare she would wake from? Why hadn't she seen this coming?

After listening to the ATIS broadcast for current weather, she held her microphone to her lips and contacted the air traffic controller. "Lake Hood tower, Piper four-three-six-one-alpha's at the strip with information Bravo, ready for takeoff on three-one, straight out departure." Her voice cracked as she spoke—she hoped the controller recognized her speech and noted its frightened tone. Maybe he'd see that as a warning sign, be alerted to the dangerous situation developing in the Super Cub.

But even if the controller didn't notice the strain in her voice, Cameron did, and he rapped the back of her head with the gun's barrel. "Don't talk that way, sound normal. I planned to kill you somewhere else, but I can still change my mind and do it right here. Keep that in mind if you get any ideas."

The burst of adrenaline provoked by that comment shot through her system at the same time the radio speaker crackled with a reply from the controller. "Piper four-three-six-one-alpha, Hood tower. Wind is three-four-zero at two-zero, gusting to three-three. You are cleared for takeoff on runway three-one, straight out departure approved."

The acknowledgment of the wind speed made her cringe. "Cameron, this is insane," she protested. "It's gusting to thirty-three knots! I've never flown in wind that strong, and if I can't handle it and we crack up, I'll be taking you with me! Why don't you just stop this shit and let me go? It'd be a helluva lot safer."

A growl from him made his annoyance clear, and he butted the gun's barrel against her ear. The earring hanging from her lobe tinkled as the steel rubbed past it. "I'm not nervous," he declared, "you can handle it. You're not going to ground-loop." He pressed the gun into the skin on her neck. "Just get going. We've got an appointment across the inlet."

The muscles in her cheek flexing, she ground her teeth. She had no choice now, she had to try her scheme to escape from him, regardless of how dangerous it would be—he wouldn't be swayed.

There was a fifty-fifty chance she could be killed during the enactment of her plan, but it was a one hundred percent chance she'd die if she didn't try. Just be cool, she thought. Wait until the moment's right. Stay cool. Steeling her nerve, she guided the Super Cub onto the runway. The strong wind battered the plane as she taxied into position, and rain clouded her vision.

"Six-one-alpha's rolling," she announced to the tower, and smoothly pushed the throttle forward.

The throaty roar of the Lycoming engine filled her ears, and the Piper surged forward. Tearing down the runway, it bounced and bucked on the ruts in the gravel, the gusty wind jerking it close to the shoulder of the strip. In about five seconds it leaped skyward, climbing like a rocket in the strong headwind.

The gun barrel smacked against her skull as the violent turbulence made the plane convulse like a man caught in an epileptic fit. It shot past the trees to the north and barreled across the gray mudflats that separated the runway from the silty water of Cook Inlet. Whitecapped waves threw themselves onto the shoreline below—raindrops struck the windshield, flattening upon impact.

As she stared at the waves, the frantic desire to do something, anything, hit her again. *No,* she ordered herself silently, *don't do it yet. Wait, it's not time.* Her gut twisted and heaved as the furious gusts hammered the Piper, tossing it up and down, right and left like a beach ball. It felt like the strong wind would twist the wings off at their roots as the plane continued to climb—two hundred feet, three hundred feet . . .

A small boat, chugging down Cook Inlet toward the fishing grounds to the west, passed under the path of the plane. White-topped waves broke over its hull, and yellow-

jacketed crew members could be seen on its deck. She
raised her eyes to glance at her altimeter—four hundred
feet, four hundred fifty . . .

She braced herself and tightened her shoulder harness—
four hundred seventy-five . . . five hundred! It was time.
She couldn't wait any longer; either her plan would work
or it wouldn't. She sucked in a deep breath, and . . .

With a jerk on the aircraft's stick, she sent the Super Cub
wheeling into a steep roll to the right. The radical maneuver
sent her guts spinning, and she was sure her stomach was
coming up her throat. The altitude indicator on the instrument panel began to oscillate, and the horizon twisted
wildly.

A scream burst out of Cameron's mouth. "What the hell
are you doing?" he shrieked, flailing his arms as he slid
sideways against the right side of the cabin.

Ignoring his panic, she continued the bank, as the over-
powering feeling of vertigo washed over her. She bit her
tongue to stifle the urge to right the plane, and kept it rolling, revolving clockwise from level to inverted. With one
hand she clung to the shoulder harness that held her still
when gravity threatened to pull her off her seat, and when
the wings became perpendicular to the horizon, she braced
herself . . .

And reached out to pop the aircraft's door open. The
upper and lower halves of the hatch swung apart like a
clamshell, and a blast of air surged into the cabin, tearing
the maps out of the wall pocket. They crackled and snapped
as they flew about the cabin, and the raindrops surging into
the open cockpit pelted her face, stinging as they hit.

The Piper was flying on its side, ninety degrees off level,
the gray waters of the inlet below appearing in the yawning
gap where the door used to be. Her shoulder harness held
her securely, but without any restraint on at all, her attacker
was thrown against the wall.

He screamed in terror and began clawing at anything he
could grab. With the slipstream outside pounding his shoul-

ders and head, he tried to anchor his arms against the sides of the cockpit, but there was nothing to cling to. In a blind panic, he dropped the gun from his hand and grabbed hysterically at her seat and shoulder harness.

With the weight of two bodies on the shoulder harness, the clips that held it to the ceiling began to spring free—she shrieked and reached for anything in front of her to prevent being dragged out the airplane. As she struggled to wrench herself out of his grasp, her knee pulled the control stick farther to the right and the aircraft's roll deepened.

In a matter of seconds the Piper was entirely inverted, its wheels pointing to the sky, its tail pointing to the cold silty water below.

She was terrified—even though ready for the plane to flip on its back, she'd never rolled *any* aircraft and experienced the unnatural effects of aerobatic flight. The sensation of disorientation was entirely foreign to her, and extremely intimidating. All she could feel was the hammering of her heart—she barely acknowledged the blood running to her head as she dangled upside down from her lap belt and shoulder harness.

Then the engine began to pop and sputter, and died with a snort.

"Oh, shit!" she swore. Regardless of her expectation that the engine would quit when the plane became inverted—and start on its own when it became level again—a cold sweat broke out on her forehead. No pilot is at ease when her aircraft loses power, whether or not she anticipated it, and she had to get the Piper level once more. She'd gotten what she wanted from the wild maneuver—Cameron had dropped the gun out the door in his frantic attempt to save himself—but she still had to get the plane flying again.

"Let go!" she howled, pounding on his arms to break loose from his death grip. "Let go of me, damn you, I can't reach the controls! Let go!" She scrambled to reach the stick, to right the aircraft, but it continued to roll. As it swung past inverted and back to level, gravity yanked him back into the plane, and he bounced down the left side of the cabin like a game piece in a pinball machine. When he had to break his slide down to the floor, he finally released his grip on Taylor and yowled as he collapsed upside down on the rear seat.

As the Super Cub leveled itself, the lighter gray of the cloudy sky replaced the darker gray of the inlet water, and up began to resemble up. She fumbled with the stick and the rudder pedals to bring the Piper to straight-and-level, ready for the sound of the engine sputtering back to life. That was the way it worked.

But it didn't that day.

The prop windmilled, with no restoration of power to the engine—the plane had lost hundreds of feet of altitude during the roll, and the inlet water washed by a mere twenty feet below its wheels. She stared at the gray inlet water right below the Piper, her eyes the size of saucers.

"Damn!" she swore. "What happened?" She attempted to engage the engine herself, turning the starter once, twice, three times, but it wouldn't react as it should. Something was wrong, it wasn't responding!

She scanned the instrument panel desperately. What could it be? In her peripheral vision, she could see the distance between the plane and silty waters below shrinking perilously.

Her panic deepened.

Yelling in alarm, her opponent scrambled up from his position on the floor and strained to reach over her shoulders. "The mixture!" he screamed. "The mixture is out! Push it in, push it in!"

Taylor gaped at the controls where he pointed—he was right, somehow the mixture had been pulled back and no fuel flowed to the engine. She yelped and shoved the mixture lever forward. The engine snapped and sputtered, then snarled to life. "We've got power! We've got power!" she crowed.

Right before the Piper plowed into the water.

TWENTY-FOUR

With a splash the Piper tripped across the water of
Cook Inlet, a gray, silty funnel spraying out from
the wheels as they skimmed over the surface. A second
later, the tires buried themselves in a wave crest and the
Super Cub flipped end over end, the wings smacking the
whitecaps like a fat man belly flopping into a pool.

"Oh, shit!" Taylor shrieked, completely caught off
guard. She hung inverted, her harness taut against her
shoulders, her lap belt carving into the flesh covering her
hipbones. The unexpected view through the windshield—
horizon above sky—contained the image of miles of water
dotted with sea foam.

His neck twisted by his fall, Cameron lay crumpled in a
heap on the Plexiglas skylight. He choked and gasped as
the water rushing through the still-open clamshell door
threatened to drown him.

"Get out, get out," she croaked, the straps of her lap
belt and shoulder harness strangling her. "We gotta get out!
The plane's sinking!" She struggled to unfasten the buckle
that held her restraints together, and collapsed on her head

when it gave way, landing her in the burgeoning pool of salty water surging in from outside.

Scrambling to her hands and knees, she shoved him to the door, yelling. "Get out! Climb out on the wing, hang on to the strut!" She grunted and swore as she tried to force him out, but he protested in a panic.

"I can't swim!" he wailed. "Can't swim, don't make me go out!" He braced his arms on the door frame.

"Oh, don't bullshit me! You're a diver, all divers have to know how to swim!" She couldn't believe he was pulling such a lame attempt to stay out of the water.

His grip on the doorframe tightened. "But that's why I never got certified to dive! I can't swim! I use my brother's equipment so I never have to go to a dive shop!"

"Well, you're gonna have to learn to swim today—" She propped herself against the opposite wall and planted her feet on the small of his back.

With a well-timed shove, she sent him sprawling out onto the wing. Six inches of water covered its surface— the wing, like the entire plane, was submerging. "Out you go!" she yelled. "Staying in here's not going to do you any good!"

The whitecaps washed over the plane and pounded against its fuselage furiously. The red rotating beacon on the top of the tail pulsed from beneath the silty water— only three feet into the murky depths, the crimson strobe was barely visible.

The frigid inlet water had saturated every piece of Taylor's clothing, as well as her hair, and its chill was starting to strip the energy from her. In the back of her mind, she knew she only had a few minutes before the thirty-seven-degree water reduced her to a paralyzed stump.

"Stay out there on the wing," she ordered him. "Don't try to come back in the cabin and get in my way. The plane is sinking too fast for me to have time to fool with you. I gotta get the seat cushions out."

She left him clinging to the strut, and turned back to the

nearly submerged plane—she didn't know if she could get the seat cushions out through that much water. With the salt spray stinging her eyes, she sucked in a breath and dove down to the cushions, her navigation hindered by the clouds of silt in the water. Kicking her feet to swing her body across the compact quarters, she groped about, trying to connect with the front pilot's seat. Finally, she rubbed across a leatherette-covered square and hauled on its edge, sensing the snaps that secured it in place start to pop loose.

With only one half of the fasteners loose, she ran out of breath and pushed herself to the surface. The sight that met her when she broke out of the water horrified her: the plane had sunk even more, with a mere eight inches of air remaining in the cabin. She didn't have time to gawk—gulping a lung-full of air, she dove back down into the darkness.

Scrabbling over the seat, she found the cushion one more time and began tugging on it frantically to extract it from the frame. Her lungs burned as she struggled—she could feel the staccato march of her heartbeat pounding in her ear like a timpani. Unable to hold her breath any longer, she tore at it in a last effort, ripping it loose from its restraints.

Blinded by the muddy water, she fumbled to force the cushion clear, but it got snagged on the clamshell door as she yanked to extricate it. Huge balloons of air followed it to the surface, burped up from the cabin—the entire fuselage of the aircraft hung below the water, nothing but a small amount of trapped air keeping it afloat.

When she kicked her way out of the plane, gasping and wheezing for breath, she saw Cameron still crouching on the submerged wing. He clung to one of the main wheels, the water up to his armpits, the waves splashing over his shoulders like breaching whales. Terror distorted his features—his face was bloodless, his pupils dilated.

When he spotted the freed cushion, he reached out eagerly, his fingers poised like talons, but it floated past him on the crest of a wave. "Come back, come back!" he howled, flailing the water behind it.

Treading water to stay afloat, she saw the cushion bob past his outstretched hand. "Grab it, damn you, grab it!" she screeched, astonished by his cowardice. All he had to do was dog-paddle toward the cushion and he would be able to secure it, but he refused to relinquish his handhold on the tire. The cushion floated off, propelled by the agitated waves.

Then, with a final gurgle, the Super Cub sank.

"Oh, God!" he screamed, with no purchase for his windmilling arms. "Help me, help me! I told you I can't swim!" He floundered toward her and wrapped himself around her torso, trying to climb on top of her to stay above the water. As his weight forced her down, she choked and swallowed a mouthful of silt as she disappeared into the gloom below.

Pounding on his legs and his arms, she strove to shove him off and return to the air above. She kicked like an Olympic swimmer in the race of her life, but with every thrust she realized she was just holding her own, not making any headway.

His knees wrapped around her neck like a vise—she thought he would choke her to death. As she locked her freezing hands on his thighs, she could feel the chill of the water seeping into her muscles, and her limbs moved like lead weights held them down. The tick of her life's timer resounded loudly in her mind—every second she remained submerged brought death closer.

When that realization hit her, a burst of adrenaline shot through her system and she multiplied her efforts to escape. Even with lungs begging for air, she pummeled violently at his legs and tried to tear them off her neck. Clawing at him, she finally connected with a tender spot behind his kneecap and he jerked away from her in pain. Free of the lethal grasp of his thighs, she shot off, her arms pushing her through the water with the last of their strength.

Five feet from him, she popped up into the air, face-to-face with the floating cushion. Grabbing it, she pulled it to her chest and held her head out of the waves while she coughed and hacked.

Nearby, Cameron was in real trouble. He slapped the water vigorously, shrieking and crying, his head tilted back to keep his mouth and nose above the surface. "Taylor, Taylor, help me! Help me!" he yowled as he spit water out of his mouth.

She stared at him for a moment, just a moment, before she made a snap decision to strike out and rescue him. Abject terror filled his expression—he was dying and he knew it, but she wasn't going to let it happen. She wouldn't be responsible for anybody's death, not even the man bent on killing her.

Paddling fiercely, she steered the cushion toward him. Once his salvation came in sight, he greedily clutched it and tried to haul his body on top of it. "No, no, don't do that!" she yelled at him. "It can't hold you and me both! Grab on to one side, don't try to float on it!"

But with a crazed look in his eyes, he pulled the support to his chest and began to dog-paddle rapidly away from her. With the help of the wind and waves, he was ten feet away in seconds, the crests of the waves already hiding his form.

She gaped at him, as she treaded the open water with disbelief in her expression—he had saved himself, leaving her to struggle for life on her own. The cold Alaskan water was stripping all of the energy from her limbs, and he knew it—there was no way she could catch up with him.

"Cameron, don't do it! Cameron!" she screamed, when she realized that he was doing precisely what he intended to do all along. Here she thought she had escaped his plan for murder by getting the gun away from him, but she'd done nothing. He still intended to kill her, but had chosen a different weapon—the icy water would do his dirty work for him, he didn't have to lift a finger.

She had played right into his hands.

As her head bobbed in the whitecapped waves, the fatigue brought on by the cold drained the will to fight from her. Her legs kicked slower and slower, her head dipped lower below the waves, she was ready to give up—Cameron had won. Not only had he engineered her death, he'd never be prosecuted for it, or the five other deaths he'd caused.

As she digested that idea, she felt lethargy take her over and her body relaxed. Without thinking about it, her legs made one more feeble kick then ceased to move. She rolled onto her back, spread-eagled, the waves surging past and washing over her face. She couldn't even spit the silt out of her mouth; none of her muscles would respond to the commands from her brain.

She was so tired. So, so tired.

TWENTY-FIVE

An antiseptic smell tickled Taylor's nostrils, and she stirred under crisp sheets, listening to the hospital sounds all around her. In the hall outside her room she heard somebody shuffling by unsteadily—most likely a surgical patient walking the halls to loosen himself up. The doctors wanted to get people moving as soon as possible after a shock to the body like surgery, as that aided in their recovery. The squeaking noise accompanying the slow footfalls sounded like the wheels of the IV pedestal the man—or the woman?—dragged along.

The clatter of plates nearby indicated a nurse or aide bringing breakfast around, and if she didn't display signs of activity the server would not drop a meal off. Lassitude soaked her body—she hadn't recovered from the fatigue brought on by hypothermia—but she was more hungry than drowsy so she forced herself to show some life by opening her eyes.

The image that filled them was unexpected.

Steve Derossett stood in the doorway, leaning against the doorjamb with his arms crossed over his chest. He still had his Nomex flight suit on—he must have come directly from the airport after his return from Texas. A subtle smile brushed across his face, and one eyebrow was raised. "Good morning. How'd you sleep?" he quizzed her.

She gaped at him and sat up in bed, swinging her legs over the edge of the mattress to run to him. However, a stabbing pain accompanied her lurch and she groaned before sinking back against the inclined bed. "Ooh, that wasn't too smart," she muttered.

"Settle down there, Miss Morgan," admonished a nurse who peered at her from behind Steve. "You shouldn't be trying to get out of bed." The woman—her name tag said "Becky" and she was the third nurse Taylor had had in eighteen hours—stepped around the tall man and placed a covered plate on the bedside table. After removing the dish's hood, she moved over to the head of the bed, fluffed the pillow, and tucked the covers back in place.

The sight of the nurse's blond hair and bright smile made Taylor want to cringe—the nurse had no right to be so perky, she thought. No doubt Becky's ebullient mood interfered with the patients—after all, this was a hospital, and sick people wanted to be able to feel sorry for themselves. They paid big bucks for that privilege, and they wanted to come home with some really good horror stories about their stays so they could rile up copious amounts of sympathy.

Backing away from the bed, Becky cautioned her charge. "No quick movements, please, Miss Morgan. You've got a concussion, and you don't want to rip your stitches out." With another cheerful grin, she edged around the Lear pilot again. "Make her behave herself, okay?" she ordered and walked off.

"What makes you think I can do that?" he cracked. "She never listens to *me*." He glared at her in mock-annoyance.

Taylor shrugged, then reached up to finger the bald spot on her head. What a drag that was, looking like a Hare Krishna cultist who'd changed his mind about getting one of their really flattering haircuts halfway through it. She could still hear the *scritch* of the razor blade as the emergency room doctor shaved a patch of hair around the nasty gash on her scalp.

"You're lucky that your head was the only thing you hurt," he chided. "You don't use it, anyway."

When he appeared to be disparaging her—rather than showing relief because she was all right—she just shrugged. From past experience, she knew his accusatory tone was par for the course. He wasn't going to reward her for pulling her toes out of a fire of her own making, assuming that would encourage her.

However, the absence of his praise when she did something clever would not prevent her from trying it time and time again.

After shaking his head—his expression saying, "Why do I put up with this?"—he moved to the side of her bed and pushed the roll-away table and her breakfast closer. Extracting her silverware from the napkin wrapper, he handed her a spoon. "Here, eat something. It's your favorite, oatmeal." He wrinkled his nose and sat down on the blue-cushioned chair next to the IV stand.

"I'm starving," she acknowledged, accepting the spoon gratefully. "I could even eat one of your breakfasts, I'm so hungry." She dove into the bowl of oatmeal, rapidly alternating a scoop of hot cereal with a bite of toast.

"Slow down, slow down. You're going to choke on something. I don't want to have to give you the Heimlich maneuver right in the middle of a hospital."

"Yes, Mother." She laid her toast down and concentrated her actions on the oatmeal. "When did you get home?" she asked, glancing up from her breakfast. "How'd you know I was here?"

"Nate was waiting for me at the hangar when I taxied up a few hours ago. He knew when I was due in—you would've known, too, if you hadn't been racing around in Cameron's Cub when I called your house—and he figured I'd want to know." He leaned back in his chair, a sheepish expression on his face. "So, how does it feel to be right? After I told you to lay off?"

She felt like grinning smugly, but then thought better. Rubbing his nose in it didn't appeal to her, as it sounded a little like he was apologizing for doubting her hunch. "Well, I wasn't really right," she confessed. "Until I knew that Cameron was the one behind everything, I thought Walter Wolverton was the guilty party. Him being Erica's ex and all." She scooped up another slug of oatmeal and stuffed it into her craw. With her mouth full she mumbled, "By the time I figured out it was Cameron, he was on to me. Then I was in a shitload of trouble."

"Yeah, I guess so. Nate told me what he knew about what happened. How did you come up with the idea of doing a roll in the Cub? That plane's not built to handle aerobatics, and as far as I know, neither are you. I didn't know you had any experience doing stunts like that." He studied her, and she hoped it was an admiring look, rather than one that meant she was really, really stupid.

She tried to salvage a small bit of her ego with her next comment. "Hey, I had to try it, even though I didn't know what I was doing. If I hadn't gotten him to drop the gun, I would've been fertilizer for the fireweed on the other side of the inlet."

He nodded, still unwilling to give her any points for her ingenuity, then blanched when another thought arose. "Was that dive into the inlet part of the whole scheme? Did you know he couldn't swim? Were you trying to drown him, take an eye for an eye?"

He looked as though he wasn't sure if he wanted to be involved with a woman who could coldly avenge the death of a friend by killing the one behind it. His expression displayed real aversion to that.

"No, oh, no. That wasn't it at all." The rapid shake of her head that punctuated that comment provoked another cringe from her. "Oh, ouch. I gotta quit that." She set her spoon down and closed her eyes for a moment.

"Anyway," she added after opening her eyes, "we landed in the drink because I pulled the mixture back and the engine wouldn't start when we leveled off. I thought I'd be able to climb away from the water once I had power, but—"

"What the hell did you do that for, pull the mixture out? You know the engine won't fire with no fuel going to it."

"Duh. You think I did that on purpose? When that slimeball grabbed me to keep from falling out the door, I anchored on to the first thing I could to keep him from dragging me out with him."

"Well, he should've had his seat belt on. Then he wouldn't have come so close to bailing out like that." He stopped to squint at her. "Why didn't he have his belt on, anyway? Did you tamper with it?"

"Yeah, right. When could I have done that?" She thought she was quick-witted, but not *that* quick-witted. "He must've thought I was going to try something sneaky and he left it off so he could move fast if he had to." She laughed, attempting not to move too much in the process. "That'll teach him to think. Here he thought he had it all figured out, but he never imagined I'd try a roll. Pretty cool, huh?"

Arching an eyebrow, he smiled. "Don't get a swollen head over it. You're pretty lucky that the crash boat got to you as fast as it did. If it hadn't, you would've drowned when hypothermia shut everything down."

She shook her head when he mentioned the rescue boat. "But how'd they know I was in the water? I mean, yeah, the ELT went off when I hit, but I doubt they got there so fast because of that. Wonder what it was." She knotted her eyebrows and gingerly caressed the hairless spot on her scalp. Even though it had been shaved only eighteen hours earlier, stubble had already come up.

Steve laughed at her confusion. "I think you have to thank the controller that was on duty at International yesterday afternoon. He recognized your voice and could hear from its tone that you were in trouble somehow. He was using his binoculars to track the Super Cub after you took off, and saw you start the roll before you smacked into the water.'' He grinned in satisfaction at her slack-jawed expression. ''Then he alerted the crash boat. He was a selfless federal employee, calling on other federal employees to drag your sorry butt out of the inlet. Never say our tax dollars haven't ever worked for *you*.''

Steve's description of her rescue made her thoughts freeze on a point that hadn't occurred to her as she lay recuperating in the hospital. Her guts seized in retrospect. ''Where's Cam?'' she questioned suddenly. ''He didn't get away, did he? I told the guy on the crash boat what Cam'd done, but I was kinda out of it by then. I don't know if anyone went after him. He's not out there loose, is he—''

''Hah!'' Steve cackled gleefully. ''Don't worry about that! Another boat came out, and they got him. No problem. Cam was paddling that damn seat cushion as fast as he could to escape, but the tide was out. He couldn't reach the shoreline; he couldn't even get any farther than the edge of the mud flats before he ran out of water. They caught him there, kneeling on the cushion in the middle of the mud. He was screwed then. Even *he* wasn't crazy enough to jump off the seat pad and wade into that goo. He would have sunk into the mud for sure if he had, and might've drowned when the tide came back in. Bad way to die, huh?''

Then his mien shifted from pleased to somber. Stuffing his hands into his flight suit pockets, he stared at her fixedly. ''I'm not sure if I should be glad you're in one piece, or pissed because you got yourself into so much trouble to begin with. You're one lucky lady. . . .''

''Well, it wasn't all *luck*. A few brain cells contributed to it, too.'' She tried to strike a dignified and intellectual pose but couldn't hold it without cracking up. Her relief at being rescued shone through the laughter like a neon bulb.

He studied her glee, then grasped her hand and kissed it like an eighteenth-century suitor. ''I don't dare kiss you anywhere else. I'm afraid I'll provoke you into doing something else you'll regret. What with the concussion and all." He grinned lasciviously. "Anyway, I guess there's no way I can hope you won't do anything so . . . dramatic . . . again, huh?"

"Well, you know me—"

"Yeah, I do. That's what worries me."